'You swine!'

'I've a good mi...
country and tea...
really means,' Cord snarled ...

'And how would you do that? Beat me, whip me—I can just imagine!'

'Not at all; there are other ways to subdue a rebellious female.'

Aline smiled bitterly. 'Well, you might not think much of me, but at least I don't use people and then discard them when I feel like it.'

Dear Reader

For many of us, this is the best period of the year—the season of goodwill and celebration—though it can make big demands on your time and pocket, too! Or maybe you prefer to spend these mid-winter months more quietly? Whatever you've got planned, Mills & Boon's romances are always there for you as special friends at the turn of the year: easy, entertaining and comforting reads that are great value for money. Stay warm, won't you!

The Editor

Helen Brooks lives in Northamptonshire and is married with three children. As a committed Christian, busy housewife and mother, spare time is at a premium but her hobbies include reading, swimming and walking her comical and very lovable old dog. Her long-cherished aspiration to write became a reality when she put pen to paper on reaching the age of forty, and sent the result off to Mills & Boon.

Recent titles by the same author:

DECEITFUL LOVER
THE DEVIL YOU KNOW
STONE ANGEL

CRUEL CONSPIRACY

BY

HELEN BROOKS

MILLS & BOON LIMITED
ETON HOUSE   18-24 PARADISE ROAD
RICHMOND   SURREY   TW9 1SR

First published in Great Britain 1992
by Mills & Boon Limited

© Helen Brooks 1992

Australian copyright 1992
Philippine copyright 1993
This edition 1993

ISBN 0 263 77863 0

Set in Times Roman 10 on 11½ pt.
01-9301-57143 C

Made and printed in Great Britain

CHAPTER ONE

'WHAT the hell do you think you're doing?' As the harsh male voice barked out viciously behind her, Aline swung round nervously, scattering the wad of papers she had been holding in a whirling arc round the feet of the tall dark man in the doorway.

'You made me jump...' Her voice faltered to a halt as she took in the blazing anger turning the cold grey eyes into black narrowed slits, and the menacing power apparent in every line of the big, taut body.

'I'll do more than that!' The man moved a step forward into the room and she shrank against Tim's desk, her dark brown eyes wide with fear. 'You're Tim's sister, aren't you?' He glanced at the small photograph propped to one side of a pile of files which showed her laughing into the camera, her thick silver-blonde hair blown wildly in all directions.

'Yes.' She straightened hopefully as she answered. He must have thought she was a burglar at first; that would explain his hostility.

'And where is your precious brother?' The black fury in the handsome face hadn't lessened by so much as an iota. 'Sent you to do more of his dirty work?'

'I don't know what you're talking about.' Aline drew herself up to her full five feet, ten inches as she glared in her turn, her heart-shaped face pale. 'Tim asked me to fetch some papers for him, that's all. I don't know who you are but it's nothing to do with you. He's informed his immediate supervisor that he's ill, but there are a few things he needs to work on at home.'

'He's not at home.' The cold voice was rapier-sharp. 'People have been phoning there for days, believe me.'

'Well, that's not a crime, is it?' She was beginning to feel furiously angry. Who did this great hulk of a man think he was, anyway? 'He happens to be staying with me, not that it's any of your business! I've told you, he isn't well.'

'He isn't well.' He repeated her words slowly in icy mockery. 'And you, of course, have no idea what is wrong with him?'

'It's a virus of some sort.' She looked at the harsh face in bewilderment, a faint unease beginning to grip her and quell the anger with shadowy fingers. 'Flu, I suppose.'

'Flu!' He gave a harsh bite of laughter that made her flinch. 'I'll give him flu when I get hold of him. Your dear brother, Miss Marcell, is in a great deal of trouble, and if I find out that you are involved, as I suspect you are, you are going to wish you had never been born.'

'Who exactly are you?' She was beginning to feel weak at the knees. She had only returned from a month's holiday in Greece a few hours before, to find Tim firmly settled in her tiny flat, pleading that the big house he shared with three friends was being painted and the smell and commotion was making him more ill. She had been deeply shocked at the pale, sickly greyness of his skin and immediately fussed round him, promising he could stay until he was feeling better and she would sleep on the small sofabed in the lounge.

'Cord Lachoni.' The deep voice fairly spat the words at her. 'Has Tim mentioned my name?'

Had he mentioned the name! Cord Lachoni. The Big White Chief. Known far and wide for his ruthless efficiency and cold-blooded business sense that had brought him from relative obscurity to the status of multi-millionaire in less than ten years. An entrepreneur to end entrepreneurs, hated and feared as well as deeply respected among his peers. At thirty-seven he had the world at his feet, a broken marriage and a string of much publicised one-night stands to his credit. A giant among men with a lifestyle to match.

'Well?' The stony hard voice was unrelenting. 'What are you hatching in that nasty little brain of yours? I can fairly hear the cogs whirring.'

'Look, Mr Lachoni, you aren't going to believe this,' she began slowly, 'but I haven't got a clue what this is all about.'

He swore softly in a foreign tongue, the meaning unmistakable. 'You're right, I don't believe it,' he said crisply, moving to stand in front of her, where he towered over her slender frame. His height was terribly intimidating, six feet six at least, with the sleek, broad-shouldered body of a prime athlete honed to perfection. She could see that some women would find such powerful raw masculinity attractive, but the dark, rugged face held a touch of cruelty that chilled her blood. He was like one of the big cats, fascinating from a distance but intimidatingly unnerving close to.

'Tim told his head of department he was ill,' she repeated desperately as tiny shivers of fear sped down her spine. 'I'm sure he'll be back at work as soon as he can make it. Our uncle works here; he said to——'

'Do you think I am a complete fool?' There was just a glimmer of an accent on some of his words, an unusual pronunciation of certain letters that, along with the bronzed darkness of his skin, proclaimed he was not English. She tried desperately to remember everything Tim had mentioned about this man as she sat with a small plop on the hard surface of the desk. The hard grey gaze had her pinned like a butterfly on cardboard.

'No, I don't think you're foolish, Mr Lachoni.' She ran her hand distractedly over her eyes, feeling totally perplexed. 'I just don't understand——'

'You don't understand?' The words were pure acid. 'Well, perhaps I can help you understand.' She stared at him with huge eyes as he stepped back a pace, crossing his muscled arms and opening his legs slightly as he stood watching her. Her heart gave a sudden jump that was nothing to do with fear. He was lethal; she could almost taste his maleness.

'As I am sure you are aware, your brother was offered a position with my company on the recommendation of your uncle.' She nodded silently. 'For a university graduate with no experience, he was given a reasonably responsible post in your uncle's department. He was obviously thought to be completely trustworthy and honest.'

Aline's brown eyes dilated with growing apprehension. There was something terribly wrong here.

'Just over a week ago it was found that a considerable amount of money was missing from company funds. Your uncle, as financial director, instigated an immediate enquiry. The result of that investigation has all but broken him.' He moved suddenly, lowering his body until his face was on a level with hers, the well-shaped lips drawn back from his teeth in an angry snarl.

'Do you know what the pair of you have done to him?' His voice was shaking with compressed rage. 'Your uncle is one of the finest men I know, and there aren't many of those around, believe me. He is a close friend as well as an excellent employee. The money is almost incidental——' he waved his hand irritably '—but what is inexcusable, criminal, is that you have taken your uncle's trust and ground it into the dust.'

'Please...' Aline felt she was slipping into a black abyss. 'Are you saying that Tim has taken the money?'

'Enough!' He hit the top of the desk with his clenched fist as he turned violently away from her, his dark face alive with searing contempt. 'Stop playing this game, Miss Marcell, or I will make you regret it. This innocent routine will not work with me. You might think your uncle is easily fooled, but not I. I've seen a thousand like you in my time and I can break you like that!' He clicked his long fingers sharply. 'It's only because of my friendship with Ronald that the police haven't been notified yet.'

'They haven't?' She felt a rush of relief that straightened her back and cleared her swimming head. 'How do you know for sure it was Tim who took your money? There must be some mistake. Big companies are always misplacing large amounts of money—computers go wrong and so on.'

'Still want to play?' The cold, handsome face was venomous. 'OK, I'll go along with you for a while.' His voice was quiet now, with a cool, silky smoothness that frightened her more than the throbbing rage had done. 'Two weeks before you so *conveniently* decided to have an expensive holiday abroad, fifty thousand pounds was taken out of company funds, unaccounted for. The next morning Tim's bank account showed a deposit for the same amount, which was then withdrawn in full five days later. On the same day that the auditors came in Tim became mysteriously ill and vanished into thin air. Your uncle had no idea where either of you could be contacted——'

'I left my address with Tim,' Aline protested vehemently, but he continued as though she had not spoken.

'It was all so very pat, wasn't it? Cleverly contrived and executed. What does surprise me is that you have the gall to come back here now.' His grey eyes narrowed into slits. 'What did you need?'

'Tim asked me to collect some files for him. He said he wanted to work on them now he was over the worst.'

'I bet he did.' His eyes were tight on her white face. 'But the worst is yet to come, my cool little dove. It was necessary to come for them in the middle of the night? The morning wouldn't have sufficed?'

'It's only half-past ten, and Tim was anxious to get started. I only got back from Greece this evening and——'

'I am not a child, so please don't treat me like one.' He moved across to stand in front of her again. 'You came at this time of night because you thought no one would be around, or, if they were, you imagined you would charm your way clear. First mistake.' His cold eyes flickered over her smooth, pale English skin and thick silver hair. 'I don't charm easy.' She looked into the cruel, dark face and a tiny shudder shivered down her spine. What had she got into?

'Your second mistake was the pure-and-innocent routine. I don't like it.' His eyes lingered for a moment on her soft full lips. 'I know from your uncle that Tim and you are twins, and by Ronald's own admission about as close as brother and sister could be. Do you seriously expect me to believe that he would do something so potentially dangerous and not tell you?' His mouth twisted in disgust. 'And what about your holiday? Your uncle tells me you have been looking for a permanent teaching post for months and merely filling in with temporary jobs in the meantime for abysmal pay most of the time. How did you manage to take off for weeks on end?'

'A friend repaid some money she owed.' He grimaced with contempt. 'It's true!' She looked at him appealingly. 'Mum and Dad died when we were in our first year at university and Uncle Ron invested our inheritance for us. When we got our degrees and moved down to London I bought my flat at the same time as Tim bought a share in the house he lives in. A friend of mine from university had run up some massive bills and was slowly sinking. I baled her out with the last of my money. It was a gift at the time and not a loan, although Jennie insisted otherwise. I hadn't heard from her for the last two years, and then she turned up on the doorstep with a new husband, who happens to be a rich Australian sheep farmer. They repaid the money in full with interest. It's the truth.'

'She can obviously verify your story?' he asked disbelievingly, his eyes watching her every expression.

'Of course.' Aline's face dropped. 'At least, she can in a few weeks. They were going on a long cruise and won't be home in Australia until November. I've got their address and——'

'Spare me, Miss Marcell.' The cold voice was quite without feeling. 'I'm a big boy now, and fairy-tales don't hold the same appeal as they used to. You were very foolish to steal from me, very foolish indeed. You will take me to where Tim is hiding now.' It was not a request.

'He's not hiding.' She stopped abruptly. Suddenly things that had faintly puzzled her became crystal-clear. Tim's unexplained relief at her return from Greece a few days earlier than planned, his absolute insistence that she go and get the files for him that very night, his haunted red-rimmed eyes and grey face—all took on a new significance now. She had just thought he was worrying unnecessarily about his work, but for a moment she saw his actions in a whole new light. She shook herself mentally. What was she thinking of? She mustn't let this cold, hard stranger persuade her Tim was a thief.

He was her brother, for goodness' sake, her beloved twin; she would trust him with her life.

She brought her chin up with a firm jerk and went to move away from the desk, but Cord caught her arm with steel-hard fingers. 'The papers?' His voice was icy. 'Don't tell me you've forgotten what you came for? Or perhaps they aren't so important now you've been discovered?'

She picked up the folders Tim had asked for with hands that trembled, and he took them from her, glancing swiftly at their contents. His face was grim. 'As I thought.' He didn't elaborate and she stared at him in mute misery. 'Now it's reckoning time, Miss Marcell. You and Tim have had your fun and now you pay for it. How much is left?'

'What?' She stared at him uncomprehendingly.

'The money,' he said coldly. 'How much of it is left?'

'I don't know anything about your money.'

He swore softly again in that foreign tongue and took her arm as he threw the folders down on to the desk, where they spilled their contents on to the floor. 'Take me to him.'

'What are you going to do?' Her voice was a whisper.

He glanced at her without speaking as he took Tim's office keys from her nerveless fingers and they left the room, locking the doors they passed through with his own set of keys and turning on the alarm in the foyer of the building. He didn't reply until they were outside in the quiet London street, the soft summer air gentle on her flushed face but flavoured with exhaust fumes and the evening smell of all big cities.

'You'll find out soon enough what I have in mind. Ignorance can be bliss.' He held her arm in a tight grip as he walked her over to where a stately peacock-blue Bentley was waiting, parked in solitary splendour in the tree-lined avenue. 'Get in.' His tone brooked no argument and she did as he ordered, sliding into the plush leather interior in a stunned daze.

He coiled himself into the driver's seat with smooth animal grace, glancing once at her white, strained face before starting the engine. 'Don't ask for pity—you've brought this on yourself, you know.' She couldn't answer, her mind was numb, and he shrugged briefly as the big car purred into life.

She was frightened, really frightened now, but a tiny part of her still clung to the hope that it was all a mistake, that Tim would be able to explain it all away with one of his infectious grins and disarming jokes. She believed in him, she *did*, no matter what this monster sitting so composedly by the side of her might say.

That hope died when they knocked on the front door of her ground-floor flat. Cord had positioned himself to one side of the hallway, and as Tim opened the door he shrank even further into the concealing shadows. 'Where's your key?' Tim sounded petulant and irritable, and as Cord stepped forward he dangled the set of keys between his long fingers.

'You mean these?'

As horrified shock, panic and fear turned her brother's good-looking face into a distorted caricature Aline knew a flash of sickening pain so acute that it took her breath away. It was true! Her beloved twin was a thief. It was unbelievable.

'You've got some talking to do, young man, and I want the truth. I've had enough hedging by your sister to last me all night. My patience is all run out, so don't push it.'

'Mr Lachoni...' Tim's voice was a weak, trembling whisper, but the granite-hard eyes held no mercy.

'The very same. Get talking.'

The next hour was a living nightmare, and through it all Aline came to one stark conclusion: she hated Cord Lachoni more than she had ever thought it was possible to hate a living soul. It was as though he was made of iron. As Tim stumblingly explained how he had got involved with a hard-core gambling set, losing hundreds of pounds in one bad night and foolishly going on game after game, week after week, to try to recoup his losses and merely getting deeper and deeper into debt, the hard, dark face had been quite expressionless. He had only shown any emotion when Tim had started to cry, pleading incoherently for mercy, and then it had been hot, blazing scorn.

'What is the matter with you? You are not a man! The boys in my home village show more courage than you at the age of ten! How dare you ask me for leniency? Do you know what you have done to your uncle? Do you? But you don't care about him. The only thing that matters to you is your own skin.'

Tim looked at his employer beseechingly as he held out his hands imploringly. 'But they said they would break my legs. Cripple me for life.'

'And so you betrayed the trust of a man who loves you like his own children.' His narrowed gleaming eyes swept across their young frightened faces in pure disgust. 'You sicken me, the pair of you. If it weren't for the strength of my friendship with Ronald I would take great pleasure in throwing you to the wolves. I still might just do that.'

Aline looked at him in sudden awareness. He was playing with them. Like a big, sleek, powerful cat with a pair of tiny, shaking mice.

'Go ahead!' She couldn't take any more of this man's biting arrogance or Tim's utter broken subjection. 'Call the police and have done with it. We can't repay the money, so you have no alternative, do you?' She was facing him now across the small room, her dark brown eyes glowing in her white face and her silver hair adding to the paleness of her skin.

'Careful, little dove. Don't flirt with disaster.' His voice was the consistency of hot molten steel.

'I don't care! Just stop tormenting us like this. You're the one holding all the aces, you've made that perfectly clear.'

'An unfortunate metaphor in the circumstances.' His voice was mocking now; he seemed to be enjoying her helpless rage.

'You...' Her voice trailed away at the expression on his face.

'Very wise, Miss Marcell. I don't allow anyone to swear at me.'

'It must be wonderful to be so pure and holy and above the rest of us poor miserable mortals!'

Tim was looking aghast at her as she fairly spat the words into Cord's face, and now he caught hold of her arm, shaking her urgently. 'Stop it, Aline. You don't know what you're saying.'

'Yes, I do.' She turned on her brother like a small virago. 'Stand up to him, Tim! You can still have some pride left. Don't let him walk all over you. Even prison is better than losing your self-respect.'

'I can't, Sis.' Tim's voice was a mere whisper. 'It'd kill me. I'm not like you. I couldn't take it.'

'As I thought.' The sardonic voice cut through their shared agony and brought their eyes snapping round to meet his contemptuous glance. 'I suspected you were the brains behind the thing. Was it really worth breaking your uncle's heart for a holiday abroad and some new clothes?' He was speaking directly to Aline now, and for the first time Tim seemed to realise that his twin was being accused alongside him. The knowledge brought a shred of colour into his white face.

'Hang on a minute.' He spoke through bloodless lips. 'Aline had nothing to do with this, Mr Lachoni. It was only me.'

'Don't start lying now!' The voice was like a whiplash as it cut through the air. 'You haven't got the nerve for it.'

'I mean it.' Tim looked bewildered. 'She didn't know. She hasn't touched a penny of your money; it all went to pay off my debts. I promise you——'

The cold, humourless laugh made them both flinch. '*You* promise *me*?'

'Please.' Tim was trembling so much that he could hardly stand. 'Listen to me. She isn't in this. I'll pay you back somehow.' He was gabbling desperately now and Aline's heart flooded with a mixture of anger, pity and love. 'I'll do anything.'

'Will you?' The hard eyes dismissed him. 'And you? Will you do anything?' As Aline looked up at the big, powerful figure towering above her he let his eyes slowly leave her face and travel with insulting suggestiveness down the length of her body. It was as though she were standing stark naked before him and it took all of her will-power not to crumple before his knowing eyes. 'How do girls like you pay their debts?'

She had hit him before any of them realised it, springing up to reach his dark face and putting all her strength behind the blow. His head jerked back for an instant with the impact, and then he remained standing as though carved in stone as her red hand-print began to glow across one tanned cheek.

'You are going to regret that.' His voice was soft but something in its depths caused her flesh to creep. 'I'm going to bring you to your knees before I'm finished with you.' He had forgotten Tim, who was standing in frozen horror behind Aline; all his energy and malevolent hostility were centred on the tall, slim girl standing so defiantly before him. They glared at each other like two gladiators about to do battle until he swung round and walked swiftly into the small hall.

'The pair of you—in my office! Tomorrow at ten.' His back was rigid as he opened the front door. 'And don't think you can run.' He turned round for a brief instant as he left, and his eyes were vicious. 'I would find you. The world isn't big enough to hide you.'

As the door banged behind him they both remained quite still in stunned silence for a long moment, and then Aline sank down on to the carpet as her shaking legs finally gave way. 'Aline...' Tim knelt beside her and dabbed ineffectually at her white face as hot tears began to course unheeded down her cheeks. 'I'm sorry, Aline...' They clung together in mutual misery for a few minutes and then Tim helped her to her feet, his young face wretched. 'I should never have sent you tonight. I had no idea he would be there.'

She looked at him in amazement. 'You should never have taken the money in the first place!' Her voice was sharp. 'I still can't believe you did. What's the matter with you, Tim? Have you gone insane?'

He flushed hotly, his attractive face, so like hers, red with embarrassment and shame. 'I know, Sis, I know. You can't say anything to me I haven't already said to myself.'

She stared into his heavily lashed eyes and for the first time saw the weakness there she had always refused to recognise before. As long as she could remember, it had been natural to both of them that she should always take the lead, and she had never questioned why. A hundred little instances that had been leading up to this one shattering moment jumped into her mind. If only she had stopped to think, she might have realised. Perhaps she could have helped him to be more strong.

'What are we going to do?' It was the same as always. He was asking her to decide, to make all the decisions.

'We're going to your Mr Cord Lachoni's office tomorrow and accepting the punishment I'm sure he'll take great pleasure in pouring out.'

'But he might call the police in.'

'Face it, Tim, he's got every right to.' Her voice quivered slightly, but she took a deep, calming breath as she put out a hand and touched her brother's pale face in a comforting gesture. 'Don't worry, Tim, I'll be there with you.'

'But it's not you who will go to prison, is it?' His voice was truculent.

'I think it is, you know.' She looked at him with bleak, cloudy eyes. 'No one in their right mind will believe I wasn't involved. I've got no means of verifying that Jennie gave me that money for the holiday, at least not in the near future, when it matters. I was in your office tonight with a handful of incriminating files... I suppose they were incriminating, weren't they?' He nodded miserably. 'Well, there you are, then. It doesn't look very good, does it?'

'I'm sorry, Sis.' He was suddenly her little brother again, although she was only ten minutes older. 'I never intended for you to be drawn into any of this. You do believe that, don't you?'

'I suppose so... Yes, of course I do.' She gave him a spontaneous hug as his brown spaniel eyes met hers in haunted appeal. He was the only close family she had besides Uncle Ron and his wife, and she loved him no matter what he had done. He was her other half. They could even read each other's minds at times. Not lately, though, she thought ruefully to herself, more's the pity!

'Come on, Tim, let's try and get some sleep.' She pushed him towards the little couch she had been going to occupy for the night. 'And you can sleep on that thing; there's nothing wrong with you except total breakdown of your little brain cells!'

'OK.' His voice was resigned.

'There's a sleeping-bag in the cupboard in the hall and you'll just have to make do for the night. The settee isn't very comfortable, but it might be better than where we find ourselves tomorrow night.'

'Don't, Sis.' His face was as white as a sheet. 'I can't take this.'

'I'm sorry.' She felt a stab of pity as she turned and looked at him before she shut her bedroom door. 'Whatever happens, we'll face it together, Tim. It's all we can do for now. There's nothing more to do and no-where to hide. You've got to face the music.'

CHAPTER TWO

ALINE remembered her brave words the next morning as they sat in terrified silence, waiting outside Cord Lachoni's office on the top floor of the huge office building. It was all hushed luxury and quiet efficiency, unlike the other floors, where noisy bustle and action were the order of the day.

His secretary looked as though she had stepped straight out of a high-fashion magazine, every gleaming, coiffured hair in place, and make-up immaculate. Her slanted cold eyes had swept over Tim and Aline calculatingly, dismissing them as of no importance after the first cursory enquiries. After phoning their arrival through to Cord's inner sanctum she had ignored them, concentrating on her work and typing at a speed that proved she had brains as well as beauty.

Tim was beside himself with nerves, twisting and turning in the deep-cushioned seat and all but wringing his hands. A strange sort of calm had settled on Aline in the last few moments as the full realisation of Cord's wealth and power had made itself felt. A numbing fatalism had anaesthetised her senses to the point where she felt almost relaxed. She expected no mercy and would ask for none.

'You can go in now.' The secretary's cool, superior voice cut into Aline's thoughts and she raised her head as Tim leapt to his feet. She stood up slowly and took her brother's arm in a firm grip.

'You're eager for the slaughter.' She couldn't stop the sarcasm.

'I just want to get it over and done with.' Tim's voice was bleak with trepidation and she felt a flash of guilt at her words. She *was* here to support him, after all.

'I know.' She pressed his arm into her side and he gave her a wan, grateful smile as the door was opened by the unsmiling secretary.

'I'm glad to see you still think there is something to smile about.' The deep male voice was as cold as she remembered, and as she looked down the enormous room she saw his big figure sitting behind the dark walnut desk. A tide of hatred rose so swiftly in her chest that she lowered her eyes quickly in case he recognised her emotion for what it was.

'Thank you, June, that will be all for now.' He coolly dismissed his secretary, who was still standing in the doorway with her hand on the doorknob, obviously more than a little interested in what her reputable employer could possibly want with two such insignificant people.

'Your uncle will be joining us in a few minutes, but I want to speak to you first,' he stated coldly as the door closed. 'You will listen to what I have to say without interruption. Is that clear?'

'Perfectly.' She met his dark gaze now and didn't bother to disguise her feelings. He looked at her for a long, considering moment, and then glanced at Tim, standing silently by her side.

'Come here and sit down.' They did as they were told, sinking deeply into the big easy chairs placed at one side of the massive desk. It placed them at a distinct disadvantage, causing them to have to look up at Cord, whose big leather seat was at least a foot higher. Combined with his unusual height, the effect was acutely intimidating, and Aline didn't doubt for a moment that that was just what he had intended.

'You first.' He looked directly at Tim, who wilted visibly. 'From the reports I've had, you have an excellent brain—when you care to use it for the purpose for which it has been trained.' Sarcasm dripped from his words, but Tim's expression lightened fractionally. He would take any praise he could get from this man, however remote.

'You will now use it solely for me, working at increased hours for considerably reduced pay. It will leave you no time for...secular activities. From my calculations, it will take you four years to repay your half of the money with what I deduct from your present salary. If you have proved yourself trustworthy and reliable at the end of that time, your salary will rise to what it would have been had this unfortunate incident not occurred. Do I take it you have learnt your lesson?'

Tim nodded in dumb silence, an expression of amazed relief flooding his face. 'Is that all?' He clearly couldn't believe he had got off so lightly, and neither could Aline. There had to be a catch somewhere.

'All?' The cold voice was mocking. 'Do you understand the import of what I have just said? You will effectively give the next four years of your life to me, young man. When you are twenty-eight you will be free to live again the way you choose, but until then you will answer to me every minute of the day if I so wish. And the night as well! Is that acceptable to you?'

Tim nodded again. 'Anything, I'll do anything, work any hours...'

The severe face broke into the ghost of a smile. 'I'll remind you of those words when the initial relief has worn off. If you are wise you could even yet turn this unpleasant episode to good use. It's entirely up to you. I have given you the opportunity, but if you fail me——' the face didn't change but the voice became

Arctic-cold '—you will find that I don't make idle threats.'

The granite-grey eyes turned to Aline. 'And now we come to your contribution, Miss Marcell.'

Tim looked from one to the other anxiously. 'But she wasn't involved, Mr Lachoni. Really, I——'

'Don't start that again!' He didn't even look at Tim as he spoke. 'I told you before, I am not a patient man.'

'Leave it, Tim.' Aline was grateful that her voice sounded cool and collected, although she was burning with anger inside. She kept her eyes locked with Cord's piercing stare, determined that he would not make her drop her eyes before him again. 'It's no use.'

'Exactly.' His voice was silky-smooth and a slight smile touched the firm, hard mouth. 'Now, as I was saying, your contribution.' Aline's chin rose a fraction of an inch in readiness for what was to come, and the grey eyes registered the tiny movement in their icy depths.

'I understand from your uncle that you have managed to acquire a teaching post, which you are due to take up after the summer holidays in...' he consulted a pad in front of him '...two weeks?' Aline remained perfectly still. 'Is that correct?'

'You know it is.' Velvety brown eyes clashed with hard grey.

'Don't sulk, Miss Marcell. It's a most unflattering attribute.'

'I can think of worse.' Her defiance was useless and they both knew it. He sighed wearily as though dealing with a difficult child.

'I've no doubt, but let's leave your thoughts out of this.'

Suddenly she couldn't bear such total surrender and she rose to her feet jerkily. If she was standing up she could take this better.

'Where do you think you are going?' She surprised a flash of bewilderment in his face and felt momentary satisfaction.

'Nowhere. I would just prefer to stand.'

'I would prefer you to sit.' He indicated the seat with a wave of his hand, his face implacable.

'I don't want to sit down.'

'Sit!' The word was a bark and for a moment she felt exactly like a naughty puppy.

'You're enjoying this, aren't you?' she hissed as she resumed her seat, her cheeks burning with humiliation.

'Oh, every minute.' The deep voice was biting. 'I can't think of a better way to spend my valuable time than chasing after a couple of kids who have helped themselves to my hard-won cash. It's things like this that make life worthwhile.'

'I thought Uncle Ron was your main concern?' It was dangerous to provoke him but she just couldn't help herself.

He fixed her with a splinter-sharp gaze for a long minute and then rose slowly from his seat, walking round in front of her and kneeling down so that his dark face was on a level with hers. Now he was so close that she could smell the tantalising scent of expensive aftershave and sensed the coiled power in the long, muscled legs as his trousers pulled tight over his lean thighs. She suddenly felt breathlessly afraid. She had aroused a sleeping tiger and she was no match for him. She looked into his expressionless face, her dark eyes huge in her flushed face and her hair a shining silver cloud tumbling to her shoulders.

'What a viperish little tongue to keep in such a delectable mouth.' His words were softly spoken but his eyes had turned deadly. 'I'm going to enjoy taming it.' She was frozen with fear and something else, a strange sort of excitement that sent a shiver trickling down her spine and caused an unfamiliar ache in her lower stomach. 'I'm going to have you eating out of my hand before we are finished.' It was more of a threat than a promise, and by her side Tim shifted restlessly, clearly out of his depth and very uneasy.

They stared at each other for one more second and then her gaze dropped before him as humiliating tears pricked the backs of her eyes. 'I hate you.' Her voice was a soft whisper and he replied in the same tone.

'I know.'

He stood up slowly and moved unhurriedly round the desk to his seat. 'When your uncle comes in shortly, we are all going to play this down. I don't know if you are aware of it, but his heart hasn't been too good lately.' As their startled eyes shot up to meet his he nodded slowly. 'I thought not. Ronald keeps it pretty much to himself. Nevertheless, there is a problem there, and I don't want him any more worried than he has been.'

His gaze flicked to Tim with rapier-sharpness. 'You will explain fully about the gambling and the reason for your stupidity, but I have already informed him you came to me to confess, which he counts as a point in your favour. You will not disillusion him—got it?'

'Yes.' Tim's voice was bleak. Cord turned to Aline.

'Your uncle completely believes your story about the mysterious Jennie and her wealthy husband, although he had to admit he had never heard of this particular friend before. He is quite adamant his little girl couldn't be involved in all this, and I don't want the truth to hurt him further.' The cold eyes bored into Aline's brain. 'Therefore we are going to lay all this on your brother's shoulders.' His voice dripped disgust. 'But you aren't going to escape so lightly, my cool little dove. You are going to write immediately to your school and tell them that owing to unforeseen family problems you are being forced to leave the country unexpectedly and are unable to take up the appointment as arranged. Any difficulties you refer to me.'

He looked at her tightly. 'You will repay your share of the money by working as my personal assistant in France for a year for board and lodging. I am spearheading a new project over there and your fluency in French will be most useful, as will your utter devotion to my every want and need.'

Her brown eyes opened wider and he laughed sardonically. 'Within reason, naturally. I wouldn't want to impinge on your high morals, of course.'

'You want a slave.' Her voice was without expression.

'A little dramatic, but I see you follow my drift. Of course, it is entirely up to you. I would mention that you and your brother are of necessity a complete package. All or nothing, as they say.'

'And the alternative?'

'You take your chance with both the authorities and your uncle's health.'

'I have no choice, then.' She raised her blonde head proudly and looked him full in the face. 'I accept your conditions, Mr Lachoni, and I will work for you for one year to the best of my ability. I will put in as many hours as you like and do anything that is not of a personal nature, but I would like you to know this.'

He waited, unmoving, for her next words, his face dark and watchful.

'I will never eat out of your hand, as you so graphically put it; I won't even let you impinge on the real me. You are a vile bully and I will hate and despise you as long as I have breath in my body.'

There was a deep glow in the backs of his eyes as he leant across the desk towards her, and a curiously satisfied expression on his face. 'I have never been able to resist a challenge.' He stretched out a large brown hand for her to shake. 'Welcome into my employ, Miss Marcell.'

As she felt her small hand being enclosed in his firm, warm grip, something akin to an electric shock shot up her arm. 'Thank you,' she said coldly. She narrowed her eyes slightly as she took in the mocking amusement lurking in the hard face. 'I hope you won't live to regret such magnanimity.'

'I think the first five words express your true feelings, Miss Marcell.' All laughter left his face as he still held her hand imprisoned in his. 'I never do anything I will regret. As you get to know me better, you will learn this.' The words were a subtle warning, and she accepted them as such as she tried to release her hand. For some reason his touch was doing crazy things to her insides.

'Just be careful.' It was as if he knew how the feel of his flesh was affecting her. 'You might be tempted to play with fire, but I shall make sure you are badly burnt. I never allow anyone a second mistake.'

'I bet you don't.' She wished he would let go of her hand. She was suddenly vitally and painfully aware of his maleness; it was raw and compelling and undeniably sensual and she could feel her knees beginning to go weak.

'I frighten you? That is good. It will keep you...in order.' She knew for sure now that he had very little, if any, English blood in his veins. No Englishman could have made such an outrageous statement in this day and age and believed it. She could understand now why his marriage had broken up. No woman worth her salt would remain with a male chauvinist pig like him!

'No, you don't frighten me, Mr Lachoni. Disgust me, maybe, but not frighten me.'

He smiled with what almost passed for delight on his face and her blood ran cold. She was suddenly aware with crystal clarity that she had walked fair and square into the trap he had set for her, and that he would make sure there was no escape.

It didn't seem possible that a whole month had flown by since that first fateful night in Tim's office, Aline thought reflectively as she opened the front door of her apartment and wearily dropped the bulging bag of shopping she had collected on her way home on to the clean marble surface of the long breakfast-bar in the small kitchen.

Events had moved with breathtaking swiftness after her agreement to Cord's demands. Her uncle had been thrilled with what he had considered 'the chance of a lifetime'.

'You're very wise to take the opportunity Cord is giving you, my dear,' he had said to her when she explained Cord's offer to him in his office under the watchful grey eyes of the man himself. 'It will be excellent experience for you, and you can always go back to teaching at some later date.' His kind, lined face had nevertheless been slightly puzzled, and she hadn't been surprised when he had called round to her flat later that same day.

'Is everything all right, Aline?' he had asked when they had settled themselves on the sofa with a cup of tea. 'You don't seem as thrilled with the job as I would have thought. You aren't still worried about this business with Tim?'

'No, I'm fine,' she had lied smilingly. 'Just a bit breathless at everything that's happened in the last few days.'

'I can understand that. It's very generous of Cord to suggest you for the translator's job in the circumstances,' her uncle agreed musingly. 'By its very nature it's highly confidential work, and you'll be working in the capacity of his private assistant, I understand?' She nodded dumbly. 'Perhaps it was his way of letting me know he still trusts our family,' her uncle said slowly. 'I know you had nothing to do with the embezzlement, but still... What do you think?'

'Yes, I'm sure that's it.' She put her small hand over his. 'Tim's learnt his lesson, Uncle Ron. He's not a bad lad really.'

'Do you think I don't know that?' Her uncle patted her cheek comfortingly. 'He's just easily led. Your father was the same. I had to keep my eye on him too. It was easier when he met your mother. She was a wonderful woman.'

'I know.' A sudden lump came to her throat. 'I still miss her so much.' She blinked away the tears; if she started to cry now she would never stop.

'What do you know about Cord Lachoni, Uncle?' She kept her eyes lowered on her tea as she spoke, slowly putting two spoonfuls of sugar into the brown liquid.

'Why do you ask?' Her uncle's eyes were watching her carefully as she looked up at last.

'No particular reason.' She shrugged slightly as a slight tell-tale flush pinked her cheeks. 'It's just that I shall obviously be seeing a lot of him in the coming months and I wanted to know what sort of man he is. Avoid any pitfalls, so to speak.'

Her uncle took her words at face value and settled back in his seat as he spoke. 'He's a good man, one of the best—hard but fair, I've found. Mind you, I admit I've only seen his good side. I'm told he can be the very devil when he's crossed.' And how! Aline thought ruefully.

'He's not English?' She kept her face bland with considerable effort.

'Not with a surname like Lachoni!' her uncle teased. 'His mother was English, I understand; I'm not sure of the nationality of his father. Italian or Spanish, maybe; I don't know.' He looked at her strangely. 'How does that affect your working for him?'

'I was just interested, that's all.'

Her uncle's face straightened and he sat up in his seat. 'Don't get any romantic notions about him, Aline. I know he probably seems excitingly different from the boys you've been used to going around with, but he's way out of your league, my love. He's had more women than I've had hot dinners, and they never last very long. I don't want you getting hurt.'

Oh, Uncle, if only you knew, Aline thought miserably, but she contented herself with a pat on his arm as she put his mind at rest, although she would have loved to cry long and hard on that dear avuncular chest. 'I'm there to work and that's all, I promise. He's the last man on earth I would ever get involved with, and to be honest I don't even like him much.' The understatement of the year!

They had chatted for another hour and then he had left, satisfied that his small world had been magically put to rights again. She had waved him goodbye with a bright smile and a sore heart.

Within two weeks she had been established in a small apartment block on the outskirts of Boilane, the pretty French market town in which Cord's offices were situated. She hadn't been surprised to learn that he had bought the block in which to house the English employees he was bringing over with him later that month. He seemed to control everything and everyone.

She hadn't seen him again since that day in his office. All the arrangements had been made through his secretary, who had given her a list of instructions and crisply informed her it was Aline's job to smooth the way for Mr Lachoni so that everything was ready on his arrival.

It was mid-September and France was caught in the grip of a heat wave. She had longed to explore the charming French countryside but the oppressive heat was sticky and exhausting, and she had been working from early morning until late each night, liaising with potential staff, organising the new offices and trying to clear any problems before the end of the week, when Cord was due to arrive.

She had grown more weary with each progressive grinding day, often missing meals completely and arriving back at the apartment as dusk touched its charcoal fingers into the sky, too tired to do anything but shower and fall into bed until her tiny alarm clock woke her the next morning. At least the hard work stopped her from thinking about England, and she had scarcely had time to give Tim a thought except on the one or two occasions when he had telephoned her.

She left the shopping lying on the breakfast-bar and had a long, cool shower in the bright modern bathroom, thankfully letting the clean, refreshing water clear her of the grime and exhaustion of the day. After scrubbing her face clean of make-up she washed her hair thoroughly, leaving it loose on her shoulders to dry in a silky-soft cloud, wrapping a big, fluffy bath towel round her sari-fashion while she fixed a simple salad with cold meat. It was still too hot to eat much. Even with all the windows wide open, there was no movement in the still, sultry air.

The strident tone of her doorbell caused a moment's panic and then she relaxed as she remembered Mrs Consello, the elderly widow whom Cord had engaged as caretaker in the apartment below her. She had asked Aline to buy some cat food on her way home and had obviously called to collect it. She fished the bag out of the muddle of packages on the breakfast-bar and padded into the hall, hitching the towel more firmly round her slim shape.

'Here's Mog's dinner...' The words died in her throat as her alarmed gaze went up and up to finally rest on the dark satirical face of Cord Lachoni, draped non-chalantly in the doorway, his grey eyes gleaming wickedly as they took in her appearance.

'Thanks, but I've already eaten.' He brushed past her as she stood frozen and speechless before him, and she caught a whiff of that familiar sexy aftershave at the same time as her mind registered the fact that he looked overwhelmingly good in the casual short-sleeved striped shirt and tailored trousers he wore so easily. 'I can see you haven't, though.'

As she followed him in numb silence into the small kitchen she saw him frowning at her meagre meal, which she had been just about to eat. 'You can't live on that stuff, and with a shape like yours you can't be dieting.' The burning colour started from her toes and worked upwards as he turned to her. 'Isn't the allowance I've made you for food and expenses sufficient?'

'Perfectly adequate, thank you.' Her voice was a stiff croak and she cleared her throat nervously—he suddenly made the apartment seem very tiny.

'And you'd rather starve than ask me for more if it wasn't, wouldn't you?' His watching eyes had an expression in them she couldn't quite discern.

'I've told you, it's fine. I've plenty of food, Mr Lachoni, it's just too hot to try and eat, that's all.'

'I see.' His voice was non-committal. 'Well, please go ahead and feast on your banquet; I don't want to interrupt your meal.'

'I'll have it later.' She whisked the plate into the fridge before he could move, and turned with a false bright smile stitched firmly in place. 'I'm sorry, I should have offered you some refreshment. Would you like a glass of wine, or maybe a soft drink?'

'How kind.' His voice was mocking her formality. 'You'll join me?'

'Yes, of course. Do you mind if I just go and change first?'

'Please don't on my account; your outfit looks just right for a hot evening at home.'

He was loving this, the rotten pig! She would give anything to wipe that superior smile off his handsome face. As her mind searched for an adequately scathing retort he suddenly took the ground from under her feet by moving forward abruptly and touching the mauve shadows under her eyes with a surprisingly gentle hand. 'They weren't there in England. You've been working too hard.'

She looked at him warily. Another trick? If she said she hadn't he would probably ask why not, and if she agreed with his statement she would be wrong there too. He read her expression accurately and surprised her still further by suddenly relaxing into a delighted chuckle. 'Oh, those eyes! They speak volumes. You don't trust me an inch, do you?' She stared at him mutely. 'I'm sorry, Aline, that wasn't fair.'

'So what's new?' She lifted her chin defiantly. He needn't think he could fool her with this new soft approach; he was altogether too seductive, too experienced

and too worldly. She could just get through this
nightmare if she kept all her defences watertight, without
allowing the enemy any foothold.

He stood watching her without speaking and she
lowered her gaze as she backed away. 'I'll go and change.'
As she sped across the hall and into the safety of the
bedroom she thought she heard him chuckle again; she
slid the bolt across the door and her cheeks flushed pink
with a mixture of humiliation and anger. He was so different from any other man she had come across. Perhaps
it was his foreign blood, she didn't know, but there was
a dark charm about him that utterly unnerved her. He
was just so... male.

After she had slipped on a light sleeveless top and thin
cotton trousers she felt more in control of the situation.
She brushed her hair into a high loose knot on the top
of her head, allowing a few tendrils to fall down and
join her thick fringe, but didn't put on any make-up.
She was going to give him no cause to think she was
trying to impress him. She didn't care what he thought
about her.

He had helped himself to a glass of wine from the
fridge and was sitting back in a big easy chair with his
eyes shut as she quietly joined him in the lounge. He
seemed to fill the room. It wasn't so much his height
and breadth, which were impressive in themselves, more
a subtle kind of dark, explosive energy, a magnetism
that was vitally male which seemed to reach out and
absorb her into a sensual awareness. She didn't like how
he made her feel. How was she ever going to work with
him day after day? The thought made her shiver, and
he opened his grey eyes suddenly, his gaze piercing.

'Is that better?' He smiled slightly as he spoke, but
her face was straight as she replied.

'Yes, thank you.'

'Relax, Aline, I'm not about to eat you. I've told you, I've already dined.' He indicated a second glass of wine on the long, narrow coffee-table. 'I took the liberty of pouring you one too. I trust that is acceptable?' The slight accent and the phrasing of his words underlined his alien heritage again, and she found herself wondering when he had first learned English. She quickly pulled her mind back from such indulgence. Keep your wits sharp, she told herself firmly; you are going to need them all to deal with this man.

'Thank you.' She sat down carefully on the edge of her seat at the furthest point from him she could manage, and then jumped as he sat up suddenly, his face straight and intent.

'Look, Aline...' He hesitated momentarily. 'I came here tonight for two reasons. The first was to see if you had settled in all right and to let you know I had arrived early, and of course to thank you for the effort you've put in over the last few weeks.'

'And the second?'

He was deadly serious now, and as his eyes fixed on hers she could suddenly see why he had risen to millionaire status at such a young age. He was a force to be reckoned with. 'We are going to have to work together pretty closely over the next few months. My French is... adequate, no more, and you are going to be extremely useful to me in a number of ways.' There was no guile in his voice and she listened quietly. 'If this relationship is going to work we have to at least communicate. Do you understand me?'

'Are you saying we call a truce?' Tim always said she could be incredibly tactless and her genuine enquiry clearly caused Cord to be lost for words for a moment. She had the feeling that was a first in itself.

'Yes.' He was as direct as she had been. 'I think that is exactly what I was trying to say.'

She looked hard at him, noting the firm square jaw and clear, piercing eyes guardedly. 'Can I trust you?' she asked cautiously.

'I rather think that is my line in the circumstances,' he said drily.

'Can I?'

'Yes, you can trust me, Aline.' His voice was crisp. He clearly didn't like having his integrity questioned. Well, Mr Lachoni, neither do I, she thought militantly.

'I would prefer that, having got this far, we now forget what has gone before and concentrate on doing a good job here. This contract is very important to me and to a number of other people who are relying on me to make it happen. I can't afford any distractions. I'm going to have to see to my other business interests from time to time, and I need someone here I can fully rely on who will understand all that is going on. Well? Can I count on your full support and loyalty?'

She considered for a few moments. In view of what he thought she had done, along with Tim, it was probably a very fair suggestion. 'Yes, I think I can go along with that.' She smiled for the first time since he had arrived and her big brown eyes lit up with soft warmth.

He became perfectly still as he stared at her, and his eyes fixed on a wispy tendril of silver hair that had drifted down from the casual knot on the top of her head. 'Your fair hair and dark eyes are a very unusual combination, especially with your pale, almost transparent skin.' His voice was slightly husky. 'Cucumber-cool but with the promise of fire within.' She stared at him, mesmerised, and he smiled wryly. 'But I suppose a lot of men have told you that.'

'Oh, hundreds!' She tried for a throwaway casualness, but her voice spoilt the effect by coming out distinctly squeaky.

'Is there anyone special in your life at the moment?'

'No.' She lowered her eyes from the penetrating stare. 'I'm not very good at relationships. Tim always says I'm too much of a free spirit. I don't like it when things get too intense.'

'A kindred mind.' His voice was dry. 'I can't say the "till death us do part" league does anything for me, either.'

'Oh, I'm not against marriage.' She walked over to the open window and stood with her back to him, breathing in the warm, still air, rich with the scents of summer. Across the narrow road to the small four-tiered apartment block there was a well-stocked orchard at the end of a huge garden, and the trees were heavy with cherries, apricots and peaches as well as numerous apples and other fruits. The air was redolent of ripe fruit, and she sniffed the fragrant smell appreciatively. There were definitely compensations in working here.

'You're not?' His inquisitive voice brought her back to their conversation and she shook her head without turning round.

'No, I'm not. It's just that I have never met anyone with whom I could remotely face spending the rest of my life, and until I do I prefer to keep my friendships platonic.'

'Hmm.' The tone was sceptical. 'Does that mean you've never . . . been involved with a man before?'

She swung round now and met his eyes. 'Are you asking me if I've slept with a man?' she asked in a matter-of-fact voice.

'No one could accuse you of trying to beat round the bush, could they?' She wasn't sure if his words were intended as a criticism or a compliment.

'I hope not.' She looked him square in the face. 'And in answer to your question that was never asked, no, I haven't slept with anyone yet. I'm not ashamed of that, strange as it may seem to you. I've had opportunities.'

'Now that I can well believe,' he answered slowly, his eyes narrowed so she couldn't read the expression in their dark grey depths. He walked over to her and, before she realised what he was doing, removed the clip from her hair, so that the thick, shining silver strands fell tumbling about her shoulders in gleaming disarray. 'I like it better down.' His eyes were challenging as he looked down at her with a small cynical smile at the corner of his mouth. 'Well, well. If you are to be believed, I see before me a beautiful twenty-four-year-old virgin. And they told me the age of miracles was dead.'

'Miracles are there if you look hard enough.'

He lifted a lock of her hair in his long fingers and rubbed it caressingly. 'I knew it would feel like silk.' He was talking as though to himself, and for the life of her she was incapable of movement or speech. His voice was thick and there was a brilliant intensity about his eyes that dried her mouth and caused her heart to beat wildly with violent, erratic jerks.

'You are a very lovely woman.' He lifted her chin with one authoritative hand as he looked deep into her dark eyes. 'But you don't add up at all, my cool little dove. What one sees is certainly not what one gets. Who are you really?' His voice was a soft whisper stroking along her nerve-endings and she felt the powerful magnetism that was at the very essence of him reach out and draw her will towards his. She had never known such strong sensuality before. It fascinated her; it was like a live entity, causing her stomach muscles to knot and a slow, rhythmic pulse start beating deep in her lower stomach.

His hand moved over her flushed face slowly, tracing the outline of her lips with one lazy finger. She could feel herself melting in weak acquiescence long before his mouth came down on hers, and when it did the kiss was as jarring as an electric shock, burning and searing her into an immediate violent response that was impossible to hide.

Her lips opened obediently as he parted them to invade the softness of her mouth, plundering the sweetness within greedily. She was lost in the overwhelming smell and feel of him, an alien need taking over her senses so completely that she was rendered helpless in his arms. He growled deep in his throat as he recognised her submission and pulled her closer into his hard body, leaving her in no doubt of his desire, and, although she felt slightly shocked as his body moved against hers, a feverish delight had her locking herself still more deeply into him when the kiss became voracious.

'Aline, Aline...' His lips moved frantically over her face and throat in tiny devouring kisses and his hands swept exploringly down her body, shaping her against him in frightening intimacy, as though he was trying to draw her body into his own.

The ringing of the doorbell jerked them apart in gasping silence, and for a moment she stood, trembling and swaying, her eyes huge and black as they clung to his face.

'I think you'd better answer that,' he said slowly as the harsh sound vibrated urgently round the small apartment, and as she turned and walked dazedly to the door on shaking legs he reached out for his half-full glass of wine, gulping down the contents in one swallow.

'Hello, Mrs Consello.' She felt more than a little light-headed as she gazed vacantly at the small woman standing smilingly in the corridor. 'I got Mog's food—just a minute.' She reached for the bag on the small table next to the door, where she had placed it when Cord arrived. 'Your change is in the bag.' She was amazed that her voice could sound so normal when the very core of her was shaking uncontrollably.

'Has she gone?' As she shut the door, the hard, cold voice bit into the air with icy abruptness and brought her eyes shooting up to meet his. He walked across to stand in front of her, his dark face tight and angry. 'For a girl who doesn't know much about men, you certainly pack one lethal punch.'

He didn't believe her. The realisation made her dumb with hurt.

'Let me give you a piece of advice.' His voice was ruthlessly callous. 'If you want to play games, pick someone your own age to play them with. I'm long since past that stage, and tonight you nearly got more than you bargained for. Do you understand? Or maybe you had bargained for it?'

He waited for a response and when she said nothing walked lazily to the door, his voice taunting and cruel. 'Don't think that this little episode meant anything to me, will you? You don't get off the hook that easily. Make up your mind that you are here with me for the duration.' He opened the door and turned in the doorway, his eyes narrowing on her pale shocked face. 'I've had more than one woman try that little number on me to get what she wants, and it won't work; I'm wise to all the tricks. If that was your trump card, you have just blown it.'

His words hit her like the lash of a whip, and as he shut the door quietly behind him, leaving her alone with her thoughts, she sank down tremblingly on to a chair with her face in her hands. How could she have been so weak and stupid? What on earth had possessed her to act in that way? Her face burned with humiliation as vivid pictures flashed against her closed eyelids.

He had thought she was trying to get him to sleep with her in order that he would feel obliged to release her from their arrangement. What did he think she was? The answer made her groan aloud as she twisted in the seat. How could she respond like that to a man she barely knew? It was so out of character that for a moment she felt sheer animal panic at his easy mastery of her emotions.

She must never, ever let down her guard again. This had been a warning and she had got out of it relatively unscathed. The thought brought some comfort as she slid into bed later that night. From now on she had to be careful, very careful. Suddenly there wasn't just one enemy to fight: the most treacherous agent had turned out to be something deep within herself, and if she wanted to survive this whole miserable affair with only hurt pride and a few bruised feelings to forget she had to watch every word, every action, and never let him guess at his power over her.

CHAPTER THREE

CORD was already in his office when Aline arrived at the building early the next morning. She always enjoyed the leisurely walk to work through the clean sunlit streets of the small town before the fierce heat of the day made moving about uncomfortable. Most of the town was still residential and the neat little houses had large gardens immaculately tended, with the odd little orchard scattered here and there, the trees alive with fruit.

She had dressed as circumspectly as the baking-hot weather allowed in a short-sleeved, high-necked cotton blouse and a long full skirt that came to just above her ankles. She wasn't going to give him the chance to suggest that she was flaunting herself at him again, she thought grimly. Her hair was drawn into a tight French plait and in an effort to efface herself she wore no make-up, totally unaware that the delicate glow of her pale honey-tinted skin and the luminous beauty of her wide, heavily lashed eyes couldn't be hidden so easily.

'Hmm . . . very demure.' He held her in a mocking glance as she paused just inside the door of his room to see him seated behind his desk, the bright sunlight falling on to his black hair and throwing the snowy whiteness of his shirt into even more contrast against the tanned darkness of his skin. He looked very foreign and very dangerous and her heart leapt into her throat, but after that one caustic comment he was furiously businesslike and the morning flew by in a whirl of activity.

To her amazement, she found by the end of the day that she had actually enjoyed herself. It had been

42

satisfying getting everything organised over the last few weeks and sorting out the hundred and one minor hiccups that had occurred, but it didn't compare with the cut and thrust of the world Cord had brought her, albeit unwillingly, into. He seemed to devour the workload, suffering fools badly and causing several small panics that kept everyone on their toes and working at full steam.

'Is he always like this?' she asked Simon, a young member of the small team Cord had brought over with him from England.

'Always!' Simon's good-looking face was wry. 'It has its advantages, though: you never get bored. His interests are so diverse and he's always branching out into some new venture. I'd hate to work for anyone else.'

Aline made no comment but her eyes spoke volumes.

'You'll get used to him.' Simon laughed at her disbelieving grimace. 'All the English crew are billeted at your apartments for the moment, so would you like to walk home with us later? We're going to change and then go out for a meal. I understand there's a terrific little bistro near by and you're welcome to join us. We're——'

'I'm sorry, Simon.' The deep voice behind them made Aline start nervously. 'Miss Marcell will be needed here a little longer than the rest of you tonight. I will take her home when we've finished.' Cord's voice was quiet and pleasant and his face was bland as he looked at his employee, but the use of her surname brought a warning reproof into his words that was instantly acknowledged and accepted by the younger man.

'Fine, fine.' Simon glanced nervously at Aline as he quickly turned away. 'Some other time, then.' He was speaking out of politeness and she knew it. He wouldn't make any more overtures. Cord had made it clear she was his own private property and by tomorrow morning everyone would know it.

She waited until the others had left and the offices were deserted and then rapped angrily on the door of Cord's inner sanctum. 'Yes?' He was sitting on the edge of his desk, reading through a report, and she noticed with a little catch of breath that he had discarded his tie and his shirt was open at the collar, revealing dark, curling body hair. His big body was still and relaxed and he raised an enquiring face as she didn't speak. 'You want me?'

'Was that really necessary?' His face was bland and calm but she wasn't fooled for a minute. He knew exactly what she had meant.

'Warning Simon off like that. The way you phrased it...you know exactly what they'll all think. I'll be dubbed as your——' She stopped.

'Yes?' There was still no expression in that cold voice.

'You know what I'm trying to say. Is this all part of the punishment? I'm not going to be allowed to mix with anyone or have a normal——'

'Don't be so childish.' His cool tone cut into her rising volume abruptly. 'I happen to have some work of a confidential nature which needs to be completed tonight. You agreed to act as my personal assistant, if you remember, and that does not mean that you watch the clock. Now, if you have quite finished the hysterics, we will start work.'

She looked at him quietly as the air breathed from her body in a silent sigh. It was no use trying to fight him; he was always one step ahead. The sword of Damocles was still poised over Tim's head, ready to fall at the slightest sign of rebellion from her. Why, oh, why had she let him kiss her last night? She must have been mad! What had come over her?

Whatever it was, it returned in full force later that night. After wading through a complicated French report full of technical data and translating the necessary notes painstakingly into neat longhand, she lay back wearily in her chair for a moment with her eyes shut. She was so tired, and this relentless heat was incredibly draining.

'All finished?' He was standing watching her in the doorway as her eyes snapped open. 'Grab your handbag and we'll go and find something to eat.'

'No!' The refusal was instinctive and she flushed as his cool grey eyes narrowed thoughtfully. 'No, thank you, I mean. It's very kind of you but really there's no need, and I'm very tired...'

'All the more reason to eat out, then,' he said quietly, with that touch of steel in his voice she had come to recognise. 'It will save you having to prepare a meal when you get home.'

She had learnt enough about him by now to know that, whether his requests were termed in polite invitation or blunt command, they meant the same. The slight accent clipping his words was stronger than usual, which also told her he was annoyed.

'Do you always get your own way?' The words were out before she could stop them and she noticed that his eyes widened for a second in surprise.

'Always.' He smiled coldly. 'Admittedly there have been times when it has proved a mixed blessing. Nevertheless I don't like to be thwarted. Put it down to my Corsican blood if you like.'

'You're Corsican?' She couldn't stop the faint gleam of interest from colouring her voice and hoped he hadn't noticed.

'Partly.' He swept his black hair from his forehead as he spoke without taking his eyes off her. 'My mother was a shy little English schoolteacher visiting Corsica on holiday when she met my father.' He smiled mockingly. 'Sounds rather like you, doesn't it?' She flushed hotly at the caustic note in his words but said nothing.

'Apparently it was love at first sight, if you believe in such a rarity, and she never returned to her homeland. I understand it caused some consternation among her family at first, but they came round to the marriage in the end. They had to. There was no way my father would have let her leave him.' The way he said the last sentence sent a chill flickering down Aline's spine, whether of fear or excitement she wasn't sure.

'They still live in Corsica?'

'My parents were killed in a car crash when I was eight. I was their only child.' She couldn't take her eyes off his dark tanned face. Suddenly the Corsican heritage was fiercely predominant.

'I'm sorry,' she said softly. 'That must have been awful for you.'

He shrugged carefully. 'All things pass.' She had a feeling he wasn't speaking the truth. 'My English grandparents came out to Corsica and wanted to take me back to live with them. Naturally that didn't go down too well, but in the end a compromise was reached with my Corsican relatives. I spent most of the time in England but had two months in the summer every year in Corsica with my father's parents.'

'That must have been unsettling for a small boy.' She looked at him as he leaned dark and still against the door post. 'Didn't you find it hard?'

'Life is hard. You can't learn that too early.' There was something deep in his eyes that made her blood run cold.

'Are any of your grandparents alive now?'

'No.' He finished the conversation abruptly by turning suddenly as though regretting having said too much. She sensed he was not used to talking about himself to anyone and felt a dart of pleasure that he had let her see a little of what had made him the person he was today.

She followed him down the corridor and found him waiting for her by the lift. 'Do you like French food?' The heart-to-heart was clearly at an end.

Once in the car—a low sleek sports job this time and quite unlike the stately Bentley—he drove through the dark streets alive with twinkling lights from the numerous cafés and bars without speaking, his dark face intent on the road ahead.

The little hotel was set apart from its neighbours by colourful gardens on all sides, and Aline was delighted to find small tables set under huge spreading plane trees, where most of the customers were sitting in the perfumed air enjoying their leisurely meal in the open. As they walked into the lights a waiter was immediately at their elbow with the efficiency that made a French waiter an artist in himself, and at Cord's request he guided them to a table for two close to a small display of sweet-smelling flowering bushes, their tiny starry flowers all different shades of red, from crimson to a pale translucent pink.

'It's gorgeous here.' She spoke impulsively, her eyes wide with pleasure, and Cord smiled slowly, his own eyes intent on her glowing face.

'I thought you'd like it.'

'Have you come here before?'

'Many times.' He didn't elaborate, and she dropped the subject but couldn't help wondering whom he had brought with him those other times. Then she gave herself a mental shake. What did it matter? He was the last man on earth she should be interested in.

While they were waiting for their first course, the waiter brought them a jug of red house wine, which Cord assured her was excellent. It was. The combination of the soft warm air, the chatter of foreign tongues faintly heard from the other tables scattered around, the intoxicating perfume of a hundred different flowers and bushes, added to the fine mellow wine, began to make Aline feel as though she were on a different planet rather than still in France.

Cord stretched lazily and one of his long muscular legs brushed against her knees. 'Sorry.' He sensed her slight withdrawal and smiled sardonically. 'You're quite safe here…' He waved his hands graphically as he spoke, his eyes wicked.

'I know.' She blushed furiously and searched for a way to change the subject, her eyes fastening on the small table. 'Why has the table got two cloths on?'

He refilled her glass before answering, his eyes slowly wandering over her pink cheeks and bright eyes in mocking perusal. 'Why has the table got two cloths on?' he repeated quietly. 'Haven't you been to France before?'

'No—well, yes.' She hesitated and marshalled her thoughts; this intimate little table for two wasn't doing her nerves any good at all. 'I came on an exchange trip when I was doing my exams,' she explained quickly, 'but the family I stayed with didn't go out much. We always ate at home and I was only here for a month.'

'That's a pity.' His eyes were dark and lazy on her face. 'I must show you around a bit while you are here.' She said nothing and after a moment he continued, 'Most restaurants in France lay the table with a paper tablecloth, which is replaced at every sitting. This is usually spread over a linen cloth, as is the case tonight. The paper cloth is ours, you know.' She looked at him in surprise. 'Take a look at some of the other tables.'

She glanced round obediently and could see in the light from the lamps that most of the French clientèle were covering their cloths with sketches and drawings, often with much hilarity. 'That's rather a nice custom.' She smiled slightly. 'If you can draw, of course.'

'You don't have to be Picasso,' he said mockingly. 'I'm told there have been some wonderful love letters and even the odd proposal in verse before now.'

'Really?' She was immensely relieved that at that moment the food arrived. Cord had insisted she try the *soupe de poisson* he had ordered for himself and she found it delicious. The tureen of soup was served with a dish of croutons, some grated cheese and a dish of Rouille, which she found to be a very strong sauce. Following Cord's example, she spread two croutons with the sauce, placed them in the bottom of her bowl, then ladled the soup over them and sprinkled a little of the cheese on top. The result was mouth-watering. As was the steak *au poivre* that followed. She refused dessert, much to Cord's disgust. The peppered steak had been thick and succulent and she had had to eat every delicious mouthful, but it had left her with no room for anything else.

She watched in amazement as Cord demolished a large helping of home-made strawberry tart with ice-cream, followed by a generous helping of his favourite Roquefort cheese with fresh bread. 'You can't get this in many places, you know,' he informed her as he called the waiter for a second helping. 'It is the best cheese in the world, in my humble opinion.'

'You certainly enjoy your food,' she remarked smilingly as he sat back in his chair, replete at last, as they sipped their coffee in the cooling night air.

'I try to enjoy everything I do to the utmost,' he said gravely, but with a certain inflexion on the word 'everything' that caused her to develop a sudden interest in the table a few feet away. She tried to ignore the soft chuckle that followed but found her cheeks glowing anyway.

'That was a wonderful meal. Thank you very much,' she said after a few minutes, lifting her dark eyes to his as she spoke, her silver hair gleaming in striking contrast to their inky black depths.

'It was my pleasure.' He spoilt his politeness by adding, 'Although anything would taste good after that rabbit food you seem determined to eat. It is only the English who can make a meal out of a lettuce leaf!' She looked at him crossly but he ignored her glare. 'You've lost some weight since you came here, haven't you? You'll melt away soon.'

She stared at him in shocked surprise, unable to hide the burning flush that coloured her high cheekbones and turned her eyes brilliant. 'You've got a nerve, Cord Lachoni, you really have!'

'I don't doubt that for a minute, but why mention it now?' He sat languid and relaxed opposite her, but she noticed that his grey eyes were sharp, like those of a big black cat.

'Oh, you...' Her voice trembled and she stopped, taking a deep breath and starting again. She might have known the charm was just a light veneer; a leopard couldn't change his spots overnight. 'You dare to criticise my figure when it's your total lack of feeling that has had me working from the crack of dawn till late at night for weeks? Perhaps I haven't eaten as I should, but it's hardly surprising, is it? I'm amazed I found any time to eat at all with all I'd got to do.' Her voice was a low hiss.

His mouth smiled although there was no warmth in the piercing eyes fixed on her face. He leant across the table and took one of her pale, smooth hands in his. To anyone watching it would have seemed a loving gesture, and his tone was soft and pleasant as he spoke quietly into her eyes. 'Methinks I've hit a nerve of yours, if the truth be known. You can't bear it because I'm not falling in adoration at your feet, can you? Have I dared to suggest your shape isn't all it could be? Tut, tut.' His eyes left her face and swept downwards, returning almost immediately to her tight gaze. 'I wasn't doing that, in actual fact. As I am sure you know, you have an excellent body.' He leant even closer. 'Let's keep one thing quite clear, Aline. You and that brother of yours have got off very lightly.' His voice was still silky-soft but his eyes were slits of steel. 'I don't like thieves. I don't like cheating, conniving women. You fit the bill for both and you don't fool me for a minute. Don't think you can twist me round your little finger as I'm sure you do the rest of the men in your life. You will keep to heel with me, little English schoolteacher, or you will be very, very sorry.'

She stared at him numbly. The very fact that he could be so quietly vicious was overpoweringly menacing.

'And another thing.' His lips curled back from his white teeth in a slow sneer. 'I don't want you causing trouble among the rest of my staff, is that clear? That means you keep your delicate little paws off gullible young men like Simon if you value your hide. He's a good kid, and he wouldn't know what had hit him.'

'What do you think I am?'

He said something that sounded as if it would be very rude in his native Corsican and she tried to snatch her hand away, but he tightened his grip until her fingers felt as though they were being crushed in a vice. 'I've told you before, Aline. We both know exactly what you are. Don't make me show you the bad side of me.'

'You mean it has been good up to now?' Some faint little spark of pride wouldn't let him have it all his own way.

'You don't know the half. In my country you would be...' He stopped suddenly. 'Anyway, this is not my country, but you will do as I tell you. I warned you at our second meeting that one way or another you would be eating out of my hand by the time our association draws to a close. Now, that can be accomplished with a lot of pain or...' his iron grip lessened and he turned her hand over in his, reaching forward and kissing the rapid pulse at the base of her wrist with his warm, firm lips '... I can be a kind master. The choice is yours, my dear. Either way it will prove a pleasant diversion for me, and offer some recompense for your dishonesty.'

The touch of his lips on her soft flesh had brought her head jerking up tightly; it was as though the imprint of his lips had melted her bones. She looked straight into his cold, scornful gaze and noted the cruelty in his hard eyes as he watched her carefully. 'And I told you at that same meeting that I hate you. You won't break me—I won't let you, not even with that army you control.'

'Oh, I don't need an army.' His eyes widened in mocking innocence and she got the feeling he was thoroughly enjoying himself. 'War it is, then. I have to admit a small part of me was hoping you wouldn't take the easy way out. Obedient, docile young women have their uses, but...' he paused suggestively '... the bad ones are so much more interesting.'

She was aware even as he spoke that he was merely taunting her with a mocking, teasing note in his deep voice, but his low opinion of her still hurt with a knifelike pain. She had to face it: she was attracted to him as to no other man she had ever met. Of all the people to fall for, it had to be a man that held her in such utter contempt.

The thought brought her head downwards to hide her eyes from that sharp, perceptive mind. I've fallen for him, haven't I? she thought miserably. Her heart pounded and for a moment she felt giddy with panic. Keep your defences up, she told herself silently; if he ever guesses you're attracted to him, you're lost.

She made herself look at him as he settled back into his seat, his eyes watchful and cold. 'If you want a fight I'll give you one, Mr Lachoni.' He was immobile; only his eyes flickered in the glow of the lamps. 'But you won't win. At the end of twelve months I can walk away from you and that will be that. Your hold on me will be finished with for good.'

'We'll see.' He had changed again; his expression was bland and smiling and he dropped a swift, light kiss on the corner of her mouth as he stood up. 'And you can drop that Mr Lachoni, by the way—it's beginning to annoy me. I'm not your headmaster. My name is Cord.'

She glanced up at him as he stood in front of her, his big, powerful figure only partly disguised by the clothes he wore so well, his dark, austere face calm and satisfied. No, she had to admit, he certainly wasn't like any headmaster she had ever seen. She had the uncomfortable notion that she had been manipulated for his own ends again, and the thought brought a tightening to her small, full mouth.

Well, let battle commence. She might have lost on points so far but she could only pray she would survive the war.

He took her arm as they left the grounds of the restaurant and she was aware that more than one set of female eyes were following them. If only they knew! She bit her lips to stop an ironic smile from showing. Those poor fools back there were probably envying her, and little did they know that she would willingly have swapped places with any one of them at this moment in time.

Aline was vaguely conscious of an unfamiliar sound as she woke early the next morning before it was light after a troubled, restless night. It was raining! She padded to the window and looked gratefully at the barrage of water beating steadily against the glass. Already the air was several degrees cooler, without the muggy, sticky heat that had proved so debilitating. She had never been so glad to see rain in all her life, and she sat by the window for an hour or so after making a pot of coffee, while the pale grey of dawn crept across the dark sky and a new day began. The extent of Cord's dislike for her had been a shock last night but she'd get through it, she told herself firmly. Never say die, as her mother had been apt to say.

There was another shock in store when she got to the office just before nine. 'Where's my desk?' She had paused in the big outer office to divest herself of her light coat and umbrella before she went through to report to Cord in the inner sanctum, and stood looking in bewilderment at the blank spot by the door where her desk had been.

'Mr Lachoni has had it moved into his rooms.' Wendy, the young copy typist, looked slightly embarrassed. 'Didn't you know?'

'He might have mentioned it.' She tried for a non-committal tone. He was clearly taking no chances on her dubious influence tainting his other staff. She forced down her rising anger. He wasn't going to get to her!

'Could you give him this list of expenses to approve first thing, Aline?' Wendy handed her a neat typewritten paper. 'He might be a bit busy later on.' She smiled knowingly at Simon, who winked back mischievously.

'Have I missed something?' She looked at Wendy's bright face enquiringly.

The other girl flushed and dropped her eyes, shrugging offhandedly. 'Not really. It's just that Claudia's arriving today with her father.'

'Claudia?' She was aware that all the English staff were eyeing her expectantly as she spoke, while appearing to be engrossed in their work.

'You know who Claudia is?' Wendy was clearly out of her depth as her cheeks turned bright red.

'I haven't a clue, sorry. Should I have?'

'Well, I thought, in view of your relationship with Mr Lachoni . . .' Wendy stopped as she realised what she had said. 'I mean——'

'I think I've got a pretty good idea of what you mean.' Her icy eyes flashed a glance at Simon's guilty face, but softened as she turned back to Wendy. It wasn't their fault, after all. They had only jumped to the conclusion that Cord had meant them to. 'Can I just make one thing perfectly clear once and for all?' She had the attention of everyone in the room now, in spite of talking in a low, calm voice; even the French staff were craning their necks to see what was happening. 'I am an employee here, just like the rest of you, nothing more and nothing less. I can understand why you might have got the wrong impression but that is what it is—a wrong impression. I work for Mr Lachoni, full stop.'

'Oh, I see,' said Wendy quickly as she flashed an annoyed glance at Simon's bent head. 'I'm sorry, Aline, I didn't mean to——'

'It's OK.' She interrupted the other girl's apology with a warm smile. 'Now, who's this Claudia?'

'Once seen, never forgotten!' Simon joined the conversation again after glancing round to make sure Cord's
door was still firmly closed. 'She's Mr Lachoni's
girlfriend and a real live man-eater!' He blew on his
fingers as though they were burnt. 'Her father is Mr
Lachoni's business partner in this French project; she's
quite a number!'

'Well, she isn't really his girlfriend, is she?' Wendy
added slowly. 'She hasn't been on the scene for months;
we thought it was all over. There was a time about two
years ago when she practically lived on the phone to him;
it got to the point where he told his secretary he was
unavailable for her calls.' Aline gathered the secretary
had been less than discreet.

'That doesn't mean he'd finished with her, does it?'
Simon argued. 'Just because Mr Lachoni took off the
heat in the office—you know what he's like for keeping
work and play separate.'

'Well, I think he realised what she's like,' Wendy
persisted defiantly. 'He's nobody's fool.'

'What is she like?' Aline tried to ignore the tightening
of her stomach muscles and increased heartbeat. She
might as well hear it all.

'A real cat!' Wendy screwed up her pretty face in
disgust.

'Oh, come on, Wendy, be fair.' Simon's voice was
laughingly chiding. 'You've got to admit she's got a lot
going for her.'

'You mean apart from her looks, wealth and avail-
ability?' Wendy was smiling now. 'I can't think of
anything.'

Aline left them still teasing each other and walked
across the room, opening the heavy door that led into
Cord's territory. He had been very explicit about how
he had wanted it arranged. The room she walked into

was merely an outer reception area with a few easy chairs dotted about a long, low coffee-table, a thick-pile carpet that almost reached one's knees and a vast array of magazines on a big glass shelf. She saw that her desk had been placed in one corner, and sighed with relief. He didn't expect her to work in the same room as him, thank goodness.

Two further doors led off this room. One led to a small lounge with a comfortable suite, well stocked drinks cabinet and its own bathroom. The other was Cord's office, a smaller version of the one in England. The two inner rooms had an interconnecting door, making them quite self-contained.

'Good morning, Aline.' Cord looked up briefly as she entered his office after knocking. 'You will observe I have had your desk moved into my outer room. This is because a lot of the work you will be doing for me is highly confidential at this stage, and I prefer to keep it that way. You will be able to engage in conversation on the telephone and translate any documents without worrying about flapping ears or prying eyes. OK?'

Put like that, it sounded reasonable, and she nodded doubtfully. If he noticed her scepticism regarding his motives he chose to ignore it. He was all high-powered tycoon today; last night might never have been. They worked at a furious pace all morning and her admiration for his astute, razor-sharp mind grew. He never allowed himself to lose his temper and seemed quite capable of dealing with several things at once.

Just before lunch when she was seated at her own desk the telephone rang shrilly. Cord had decided that all his calls would pass through her first, and the female voice on the other end of the phone sounded slightly annoyed at the delay.

'Mr Lachoni, please.' It was an order.

'Certainly. Who shall I say is calling?'

'Just put me through, will you?' The low, heavily accented voice dared her to argue. 'He is expecting my call.'

'I'm sorry, but I have to ask your name first.' Aline felt the hackles on her neck rise at the cool, authoritative tone.

There was a long silence and then, 'It's Miss Asvana, Claudia Asvana. Satisfied?'

'Just a moment.' Aline found her stomach was twisting as she buzzed Cord, who took a few moments to pick up his own phone. Claudia's voice had been distinctly ugly. 'There's a Miss Asvana on the line and I'm afraid she isn't too pleased with me.' Aline felt it was prudent to state her case first. She had the feeling Claudia wouldn't be too choosy about describing her actions.

'Claudia? What's the matter with her? What have you done now?' His voice was low and irritable and Aline held on to her temper with considerable effort.

'I haven't done anything. She demanded to be put straight through to you and I told her I had to ask for her name first. You told me——'

'Yes, yes, I know what I told you,' he interrupted her impatiently. 'However, in Claudia's case you could have put her through. She isn't the sort of woman to be kept waiting.'

'Oh, I see.' Aline knew she was going to regret her next words but no power on earth could have prevented her from speaking. 'Well, perhaps if you would like to let me have a list of your girlfriends with high priority, and audiotapes of their voices so I can recognise them without asking their names, I won't make the same mistake again.'

There was absolute quiet for a second and then Aline heard the phone in his office clatter on to his desk, and the door was flung open almost in the same instant. He stood glowering at her in the doorway and she raised her head defiantly to stare him straight in the face, forcing her mouth into a sweet false smile as she did so. 'Are you ready to receive her call now?'

They eyed each other for a full minute without speaking and she willed herself not to look away. She was in the right this time; he wasn't going to browbeat her into some kind of pathetic doormat! She had prepared herself for the onslaught, when he completely took the wind out of her sails by bursting into loud, unrestrained laughter, his face alight with delighted surprise.

'Good for you, girl.' His voice was warm and apologetic. 'It's been a long morning and I was quite in the wrong. You were absolutely right not to put her through. Give me a minute and then I'll smooth the ruffled fur.' He closed his door again and a few moments later picked up his extension. She could just imagine Claudia assuming she had engineered the delay and didn't try to speak to her again, merely putting her straight through with a small sigh of thankfulness.

What a strange man! She lay back in her seat wearily. She would never understand him; his reaction to her defiance had been the last thing she had expected but showed a strength of character she didn't want to admit to herself. Her father had always maintained it was only truly great men who could admit they were wrong, and she didn't want to think of Cord in that way; she wanted to dislike him. It was the only way she knew to protect herself.

By evening the rain had stopped and a watery golden sun was peeping hesitantly from behind soft pink clouds. Cord had remained closeted in his office all afternoon, for which she was grateful. It had given her time to marshal her defences again.

She was just tidying her desk before letting him know she was leaving when the outer door was flung open without a preliminary knock. She stared in amazement at the woman who stood framed in the opening, quite immobile and still, as though posing for a photograph. The woman spoke.

'You must be Aline.'

She recognised the voice immediately. 'Yes, that's right.' She smiled politely but there was no answering warmth in the cold, beautiful face watching her so intently. Two things registered simultaneously as the woman moved to stand just in front of her desk. The first was that Claudia—because that was undoubtedly who it was—was strikingly lovely, with a cool, unusual beauty which she could appreciate men would find irresistible. The second was that if it weren't so ridiculous she could almost have sworn it was hatred glowing in the pale, almost opaque blue eyes that were fixed on her face.

Claudia Asvana was tall, almost six feet, with a slim, perfectly shaped lithe figure that was voluptuous where it mattered. She radiated cool, contained elegance from the top of her carefully styled russet-red hair to the tips of her exquisitely shod small feet. Her large slanted eyes dominated her face, not so much because of their shape or heavily lashed lids, but because of their strange, almost cloudy lack of colour. They were of such a light blue as to appear a tinted pearl, with a hard, shining luminescence in their icy depths that was quite unnerving.

'Next time I call, you *will* put me straight through. I'm not some little office girl whom you can put on pause.' For a moment Aline wasn't sure if she had heard correctly. The red-painted mouth had hardly moved but the low words had been hissed venomously through thin, taut lips.

'I'm sorry, Miss Asvana.' Aline brindled at such unjustified malevolence but forced herself to speak calmly and quietly. 'I was merely following Mr Lachoni's orders.' She glanced away as she finished speaking, pretending to sort some papers on her desk. The older woman's unblinking reptilian gaze was making her feel dizzy.

'You will be sorry if you cross me! Just remember, you only work here. I can have you dismissed like that!' Claudia sharply snapped long white fingers, on which several rings glittered brilliantly. 'Bear that in mind next time you get ideas above your station.'

Aline glanced up quickly. There was a subtle innuendo in the vicious voice that led her to suspect they were discussing more than just the telephone call. For some reason Claudia Asvana was uneasy about her relationship with Cord. How ironic! If Aline were the last female on earth he still wouldn't want her.

'Perhaps you would like to discuss the matter with Mr Lachoni?' Aline kept her voice and face bland, and Cord noticed both as he opened his door in time to catch Aline's last few words.

'Discuss what with Mr Lachoni?' His penetrating gaze whipped over both women and for a brief second there was an awkward pause, but then Claudia smiled sweetly, opening her arms in an affected gesture as she moved forward.

'Darling... It's been so long. I just couldn't resist coming to see where my grumpy old bear works.' She turned as she reached Cord, who hadn't moved a muscle, slipping her arm through his and giving Aline a bright smile that didn't reach those deadly eyes. 'I was just explaining to your little secretary that she needn't be so formal with me another time. We're old friends, aren't we...?'

Cord gently disentangled the clinging arm and pro-
pelled Claudia forward into his office, nodding briefly
at Aline as he turned to follow her. 'Aline is not my
secretary as such, Claudia. I thought I had explained her
position this morning. She is my personal assistant, involved mainly on——'

The door shut on his cold voice and Aline let out a
long deep breath as she stood up on legs that were suddenly shaky. The growing conviction she had had for
the last few days that Tim had landed the best part of
this deal flowered into full-blown certainty.

'Thank you very much, Tim,' she muttered testily as
she shrugged uncomfortably into the coat still damp from
the morning's torrential downpour. 'You're going to have
your work cut out making this up to me.' She felt desperately homesick and very alone. She would by now
have been engrossed in her new teaching job in England
that she had waited so long for, working with children,
which she loved, instead of struggling with reams of
paperwork, meeting strange new people and painfully
typing out the odd piece of correspondence that was too
confidential for the normal staff to deal with, with two
fingers, on a typewriter that was a foreign entity to her
inexperienced hands. She blinked back the tears of self-
pity that were pricking at the backs of her eyes. She
couldn't cry here; it would have to wait until she got
home to her apartment.

'Where are you off to?' The deep voice from the
doorway brought her head jerking round. 'I've told you
before, when I ask you to stay late I will take you home.'

It was quite clear from Claudia's outraged face behind
Cord what she thought of this arrangement, and she
walked past him stiffly, pausing to touch his arm in
farewell. 'I'll see you later, then, at the house. Daddy
wants dinner for eight, so come early in time for drinks.

He said to bring the reports from the Italian vineyards so we can compare them with ours. Bye, darling.' She was gone in a wave of expensive perfume and high, clicking heels, with one poisonous glance at Aline.

Aline looked at Cord ruefully. 'She doesn't like me.'

'Don't be ridiculous.' He looked at her coldly. 'There is nothing to like or dislike.'

Well, that's put me in my place, Aline thought wryly as she waited while he locked the offices and set the alarms. He didn't speak again until they were seated in the car and then he turned to her without starting the engine. 'Why were you looking so miserable just now?'

The question was so totally unexpected that for a moment she just stared at him dumbly, lost for words. 'Was I?'

'Those eyes are killers.' He touched her flushed cheek with one musing finger, his dark face sombre. 'Well?'

'I suppose I was just feeling a bit homesick,' she prevaricated, letting her eyes fall away from his intent gaze. 'I had a long letter from Uncle Ron yesterday, and what with one thing and another...'

'Poor baby...' There was a thick velvet note in his voice that made her body melt while at the same time her mind screamed that he was playing with her again. She was horribly aware of the big, muscled body so close to her in the tight confines of the sports car, the breadth of his wide shoulders and the leashed power in that male frame. The smell of him filled her nostrils and she felt that trembling in the pit of her stomach which his nearness always managed to provoke.

'I'm all right.' She tried to be matter-of-fact but the slight quiver in her voice betrayed the tears in her lowered eyes.

'What's this?' He lifted her chin with one hand to look deep into her dark swimming eyes, and for a moment there was an indefinable expression softening the hard face that almost caused her heart to jump out of her chest. It was gone in an instant and she couldn't have put a name to it. A shutter came down over the grey eyes.

'More games?' The stony voice was suspicious, but for once Aline felt too weary and heartsore to retaliate. It had hurt more than she would have thought possible to see him with Claudia, and tonight she was beyond any quick repartee. His eyes bored into hers as he held her face imprisoned in his hand and the two of them froze, scarcely breathing, as the air around them grew heavy with waiting.

'Aline...' His voice was a soft groan but he didn't move, his gaze deepening and holding hers as though he would look into her very soul. 'Who are you?' he asked huskily, and his voice had a throb of pain in its depths. 'Who are you really? My heart tells me one thing but common sense tells me something else. I thought after thirty-seven years on this planet I had the female sex all taped, but I don't know...' He shook his black head slowly. 'You're either a superb actress or——' He stopped abruptly.

'I'm just me,' she whispered shakily, the tears shining like minute crystals on her dark lashes. 'I didn't want any of this to happen; please understand...'

His eyes were dark and glittering in the cool grey dusk that had turned the world outside the car into a mass of bottomless shadows. He seemed as though he was fighting some difficult internal battle as he drew back slightly, letting his hand fall from her face. '*I don't* understand you, Aline, that's the trouble.' His face was unsmiling and tight. 'But I will. I promise you that. Before this thing is finished I will know exactly what makes you tick.' There was a hard warning in his words and she shivered slightly, depression settling on her like a heavy shroud.

He started the engine savagely without saying any more, his face harsh as he manipulated the long, low car out of the small car park and on to the main thoroughfare.

Neither of them noticed the small white sports car pull out from the concealing shadows behind them, following at a discreet distance all the way back to Aline's apartment building. Claudia's smooth face was cold and grim as she sat behind the wheel with her eyes burning tightly on the car in front, and no one, at that moment, would have called her beautiful.

CHAPTER FOUR

'COMING for a swim after work?' Simon asked Aline invitingly with Wendy nodding encouragement in the background. The workload had lessened slightly over the last few days and Aline had been leaving on time with everyone else, often wandering back to the apartment block through the quiet, lazy streets of the small town with the rest of the English crowd, the soft, warm September air sweet to her nostrils.

There was a group of them that often stopped off to eat on the way home now, feasting on warm, oven-fresh croissants and small roasted white fish wrapped in herbs and lemon, always finishing the meal with a glass or two of kir, a local drink consisting of blackcurrant liqueur with white wine.

Aline found to her surprise that she was beginning to settle into a pleasant routine, the desperation she had felt at first drifting into the background.

Cord had been polite but distant since the conversation in his car and Claudia was very much in evidence, arriving unexpectedly at all times of the day, her slanted pale eyes ever-watchful and her tongue acidly biting, unless Cord was present, when she was all sweetness and light. Aline ignored her as much as possible, which she sensed grated on the other woman unbearably, but it was the only way she could cope with Claudia's increasingly spiteful contemplation and retain her equilibrium.

'Be ready at five,' Simon continued after she had nodded her acceptance, his voice trailing to a halt as

Cord appeared at her elbow, his handsome face set in its usual austere lines.

'Do I take it you are making plans for tonight, Aline?' he asked smoothly, totally ignoring Simon, who melted away into the background.

'Yes.' She pushed back her mane of thick blonde hair as she spoke. She had overslept that morning and hadn't had time to braid it into its usual submission. It fell in shimmering silver waves to just below her shoulders, darkening her eyes into deep black pools and high-lighting the unblemished smoothness of her clear skin.

'I'm sorry, but I shall need you here until quite late. I have two prospective buyers coming at three and the negotiations could prove arduous.' His cold grey eyes lingered on her mouth for an instant before he turned sharply and walked away, shutting the door to his offices with a slight bang.

'I don't know how you stand him,' Wendy said indignantly from her corner. 'He treats you like a slave half the time.' Aline smiled but said nothing as she turned away. A slave. Wendy had hit the nail on the head without realising it. She remembered their conversation in his office that day in England. This was his way of reminding her of her obligations. She wasn't here to enjoy herself or make friends; she was his slave.

At seven that night the meeting was still in full swing, and it was a full hour later before both parties felt they had reached a satisfactory compromise. When the two Frenchmen had left after long and courteous farewells, Cord leant back in his seat, stretching lazily with a small sigh, his muscles taut against the thin cotton of his shirt. Aline looked away hastily; the sight of that magnificent body outlined so clearly under the fine material made her oddly breathless.

'You can see I *did* need you here?' She looked at him spread out tiredly in the big leather chair, a lock of jet-black hair flopping casually on to his brow. He was undeniably and heart-stoppingly attractive.

'Yes, of course,' she said carefully.

'I got the impression that your friends out there thought I was being unfair.' He nodded in the general direction of the main offices and she flushed slightly.

'Not at all,' she lied quickly—too quickly.

'No?' His smile was chilling. 'But then they are not aware of the true facts of your sudden appearance in my company, are they?'

'Neither are you, as it happens.' She stared at him proudly as his eyes narrowed.

'Still protesting your innocence?' His voice was lazy. 'I would have thought you would have been tired of that one by now.'

'I never find the truth tiring.'

'*Touché*, my dear Miss Marcell. I am too weary to bandy words with you tonight.' He straightened in his chair as he spoke and stood up. 'Get your jacket; we're going to eat.'

She knew better than to argue, and followed him silently out to the car. He gave her one swift enigmatic glance as she leant back in the soft leather seat with a tired little sigh, and then the powerful engine purred obediently into life.

He surprised her by driving past the main thoroughfare of small restaurants and cafés where people were beginning to congregate, and still on past the neat little houses and well tended gardens beyond. She risked a darting glance at his hard profile but his face was quite expressionless as he concentrated on the road ahead, his broad, darkly tanned hands resting lightly and competently on the steering-wheel. She looked at them for a moment, remembering the feel of them on her skin, and a small shudder caused her to move restlessly in her seat.

They drove for some twenty minutes, out through the far side of the town and into the low rolling hills that faded into blackness once they left the lights of civilisation behind. Once or twice the road passed over small trickling streams and she caught sight of a low stone-built farmhouse standing on the bank in the distance, its lights a beacon in the darkness. She longed to ask him where he was taking her, but some perverse sense of pride wouldn't let her. The darting glances increased, however, in line with her nervousness, and eventually he spoke, his voice derisive. 'Do relax, Aline. I haven't spirited you away for some dark purpose of my own.'

She squirmed with embarrassment but said nothing, and a sardonic, mocking smile touched the cruel mouth for a moment. 'Sometimes you almost have me believing you are as innocent as you claim, but only sometimes...' He raised his hand to check her reply. 'I just couldn't face the thought of sitting in a restaurant making polite conversation when what I really need is a long cool shower. I'm hot, I'm tired and I'm not in the mood for people. I'll cook for us when we're both freshened up.'

'You'll cook?' Her voice was a faint squeak and now he laughed outright at her severely shaken composure.

'Yes, I'll cook,' he affirmed mockingly. 'I do cook, you know—rather well, so I'm told.'

Aline felt the sense of trepidation that had been growing steadily for the last few miles take a giant step forward.

'Look, I really don't think——' she began on a slightly desperate note, and he interrupted her brusquely.

'That's fine, don't think; I like it better that way.'

She flung him a scathing glance that was completely wasted, as he had both eyes on the dark road ahead. 'You're the most ignorant, overbearing——'

'Please, Aline.' His voice was weary now. 'I've heard all this before, so just shut up like a good little girl and behave yourself.'

'Oh!' She writhed in impotent fury and then sat in rigid silence until eventually the road turned sharply downhill and Cord manoeuvred the car into a small opening that she thought at first was a narrow lane, and then realised was a long private drive leading to what looked like a huge house in the distance.

'I've rented this place for a few months. It's quite comfortable.' It was the sort of classic understatement that she had come to expect from him. She hadn't been aware that they were travelling towards the coast, but as the lights flooded on, automatically lighting up the magnificent stone-built mansion, she saw that the huge, lawned garden led down to a small private beach of soft white sand.

Cord turned off the engine and as the sound died away she could hear the soft lapping of tiny waves on to the beach through the open car windows. 'The house has only been built a few years, but it was modelled on an old château in Loches that was built in the fifteenth century.'

'It's very... imposing.' The splendour had quite taken her breath away. 'I wouldn't have known it wasn't authentic.'

'The owner would be very relieved to hear you say that,' Cord replied drily. 'He spent over a million to ensure just that very thing. Would you like to swim?' He saw her eyes fixed longingly on the shoreline.

'I didn't bring anything...' She gestured to her body and he smiled slowly.

'I can find you a costume if you insist on wearing one. It's quite safe; there's a long slope to deep water and no submerged rocks, just a few shells and suchlike.'

'I'd love to.' She couldn't keep the eagerness from showing in her face and he looked at her intently, that curious expression she had noticed once or twice before on his face again.

'Swimming in the sea is so much better than a swimming pool,' she explained. 'Mum and Dad used to take us to the Cornish coast every summer for a month or so; we used to hire a cottage and . . .' Her voice trailed away as she remembered those happier, carefree days, and he registered the sudden sadness that turned her eyes black.

'You don't mind getting your hair wet?' He was trying to lighten the mood and she rose to the occasion with a small giggle.

'No, it soon dries.'

'Thank goodness you aren't one of those women who squeal and run for cover if a drop of water lands on their face.' His voice was quietly cynical and he clearly had someone specific in mind. She hoped, unkindly, that it was Claudia.

'Come on, let's see what we can find.' He took her hand in a light, casual grip as they went up the circular stone steps, and her heart thudded against her chest. Stop it, stop it, she cautioned herself drily—you know it doesn't mean a thing.

As Cord unlocked the massive oak door and ushered her through, clicking on an internal light as he did so, she stopped just inside the doorway, spellbound. 'It's absolutely beautiful.'

'Yes, it is.' His voice had lost its usual blasé note as he spoke and when she looked up and met his dark gaze she saw that his eyes were fixed tightly on her face. 'Very beautiful...'

She smiled nervously and moved further into the enormous hall, the floor of which was a series of beautifully worked pictures in intricately tiny tiles. There were several chaises-longues scattered against the walls, which were hung with ageing tapestries, their colours fading but their charm breathtaking.

'Is the rest of the house like this?' She looked at him with enormous eyes and he laughed softly, his eyes teasing.

'No, I have to admit it's not. I wanted to impress you, and this hall takes some beating on first sight, don't you think?' She nodded silently. 'The owner had free sway here and thoroughly indulged himself, but his wife stepped in on the other rooms. She said she preferred to live in the twentieth century, with fitted carpets and all mod cons! The sitting-room to the side here is very comfortable, and the french doors open directly on to the garden. I spend most of my time in here.'

It was a lovely room. A beautiful stone fireplace took up half one wall, logs piled high in readiness for chilly evenings, and, although the furniture was obviously antique and the pictures adorning the tall walls originals, the overall effect was one of luxurious warmth.

'Are all the other rooms as gorgeous?' She almost whispered the question and he smiled suddenly, taking hold of the hand he had relinquished when they first came in.

'Decide for yourself.' He took her on a conducted tour of the huge house, and by the time he had finished her head was buzzing, not just with the magnificence of the endless rooms she had seen, but more with the feel of his flesh against her hand and the compelling maleness of the big body at her side.

'Now, then.' They had finished at one of the guest bedrooms that was a dream of cream and gold with a huge four-poster bed draped in soft silk. 'There might be something to fit you in there.' He pointed at the large walk-in wardrobe to one side of the en-suite as he walked towards the door. 'Find something that fits and then join me in the sitting-room.'

'I shall get lost.' She felt very small and defenceless in the middle of the huge bedroom, and he laughed softly from the doorway as he took in the wide eyes and tremulous lips.

'I shall find you.' He looked very dark and foreign standing against the pale cream of the door. The English side to him had melted away and he was all Corsican, black and powerful and vitally male, his strength so tangible that she could almost reach out and touch it.

'I must be mad, completely and utterly mad. How did I get here? Why didn't I stop this?' She found she was muttering grimly to herself as she rifled through the drawer of swimwear, each tiny piece of clothing more flimsy than the one before. 'I can't wear any of this.' She grasped her middle with crossed arms and rocked gently back and forth for a moment, trying to calm the panic that was threatening to overwhelm her. 'You'll be all right, you'll be all right.' They'd have to lock her away before this nightmare was finished! The thought of appearing before him so scantily clad was causing her cheeks to burn with wild colour and her hands numb with cold.

She changed into the most discreet swimming costume she could find after several agonising minutes, tying her hair into a high sleek pony-tail with a choice from a stock of ribbons she found in another drawer. She pulled a long towelling robe over her slight figure before she left the room, hugging it to her as she negotiated her way downstairs, feeling more shy and gauche than she had ever done in the whole of her twenty-four years.

He was sitting waiting for her when she entered the sitting-room, his brown muscled body bare except for a pair of brief—very brief—swimming trunks. He followed her dazed eyes and smiled slowly. 'I don't usually bother,' he said lazily, indicating the small piece of cloth round his loins, 'but I didn't want you to run screaming from the house at this time of night. People might get the wrong impression.'

She smiled weakly. 'I doubt it. You're pretty remote here.'

'There is that.' His eyes narrowed mockingly. 'Did you find a costume that fits? I know Sandy normally keeps a stock in each room.' His gleaming eyes dared her to remove the robe.

'Sandy?' She clutched at the name like a drowning woman to a straw.

'Sandy and Mitch, the couple I rent the house from. They are old friends; Mitch and I go way back. He's gone off to do a bit of scuba-diving in the West Indies and Sandy's gone with him. She recently had a miscarriage and Mitch thought a long break would do her good. She was in a pretty bad way.'

'Oh, I see.' As he got lazily to his feet she felt her breath stop somewhere in the middle of her throat and solidify into a small, hard knot. Clothed, his body was tempting; almost naked, it was magnificent. There wasn't an ounce of surplus flesh anywhere on that tall, lean frame, just hard, trained muscle that gave his great height added power and brought a new dimension to the term 'awe-inspiring'.

'Shall we go?' He took her arm and drew her towards the full-length doors that led into the garden, and Aline willed herself not to betray the way his light touch was burning her flesh. She suddenly had the uncomfortable feeling that this night was going to be a very long one, and remembered his cold warning of a few weeks ago. 'I'm going to have you eating out of my hand before we are finished.' It was no accident that he had brought her to this deserted house tonight; it was a cold-blooded exercise on his part to subjugate her, mind and body, and she must be on her guard at all times. This man was not her friend and he was dangerous, never more so than when he was relaxed and amiable, as now. If she forgot that it would be at her own peril.

'You can leave your robe there; the water doesn't come up any further.' His hard eyes were dark with amusement as he turned at the water's edge to see her standing hesitating a few yards away, nervously flicking toefuls of sand as she gazed along the empty stretch of white beach. He had sensed her discomfiture and was enjoying every moment, the swine! Aline thought balefully.

'Fine.' She took a deep breath and let the robe slip off her body, moving down to join him as she did so with natural grace.

'Nice; very, very nice.' She didn't pretend not to understand what he meant. His eyes swept approvingly over her body in the cutaway costume, which showed her long, slim legs off to full advantage, up over the narrow waist and full, high breasts, and rested for a moment on her flushed face. 'Ready to swim?' he asked softly, and she nodded coldly, horrified to find that his warm gaze had caused her breasts to thrust tightly against the black silk of the costume, their tips turned into small hard peaks.

She waded into the icy water with a small catch of her breath as his light, dry chuckle sounded behind her. 'I hate you, Cord Lachoni,' she muttered bitterly as she began to swim with firm, strong strokes. 'You know exactly what you are doing to me and you're enjoying every minute of it.'

The water was wonderfully cold and silky-soft against her hot skin, and within a few minutes Aline had forgotten everything but the thrill of feeling her body cut effortlessly through the blue-black depths as the tiny waves bobbed against her in rhythmic harmony.

'You swim very well.' There was a definite note of surprise in the cool, deep voice at her side, and, turning, she met Cord's grey gaze. 'More like a man.'

'Is that supposed to be a compliment?' She couldn't stop her voice from being tart in view of what had gone before, and he was quick to notice.

'Don't tell me you're a feminist as well—I really couldn't take it.'

Although part of her knew he was just teasing, she couldn't help responding to the gentle disapproval in his voice, although she tried to tone her voice into light blandness.

'If your definition of a feminist is a woman who knows her own value and is happy with it, then yes, that's exactly what I am.' The effect of her words was slightly spoilt when an errant wave brought a gush of salt water spilling into her open mouth, causing her to choke and splutter helplessly for a few moments.

He waited until she had recovered, treading water slowly at her side while his glittering eyes narrowed in the white blur of his face. 'You really are something else, aren't you?' Any trace of amusement was gone from his voice and the words were bitten out between clenched teeth. 'Don't you have any remorse for the way you behave? Ever? What sort of woman are you, for crying out loud? I thought I had met the best of them in my time, but you sure take the biscuit. Isn't there even a trace of guilt in there somewhere about your uncle?'

'I've told you and told you, I haven't done anything,' she said desperately as a chill that had nothing to do with the temperature of the water swept down her spine. 'I wasn't part of the embezzlement; I don't want your money...' Her voice trailed off as she met the sardonic force of the stone-cold eyes a few inches from her own.

'I'd have to be in my second childhood to believe that. Even if what had happened in England had been a figment of my imagination, which it sure as hell wasn't, the way you blow hot and cold out here with the male sex in general indicates more about you than you realise.'

She stared at him in amazement; his words were so blatantly unfair that for a moment she was speechless with surprise. 'You might be good at the love game, little dove, but I hate to tell you, you aren't that good. No one takes Cord Lachoni for a ride twice. You don't fool me for a minute.'

He had dived beneath the surface of the water before she had gathered her wits sufficiently to reply, his long, lean body a white blur in the inky darkness of the rippling waves. The bright light from the powerful lamps on the beach was less intense out here, but still strong enough for her to catch the male grace that turned his fluid movements into the subterranean dance of a big, sleek fish perfectly at home in its environment.

'Believe what you want.' She was talking to the warm night air and suddenly the impromptu swim had lost its magic. She swam slowly back towards the lights, wishing with all her heart that she had never heard the name of Cord Lachoni.

He joined her a few minutes later on the warm sand where she was sitting waiting for him, his body wet and shining from the sea and his muscles gleaming as they moved under his firm brown skin. 'Hungry?' His voice was even and his gaze was friendly as he reached down a hand to pull her up. It was as though their previous conversation had never taken place.

'A little,' she said coolly, looking at him warily as they walked towards the house, trying to match his casualness but burningly aware of the powerful male body sauntering with unhurried animal grace at her side. The night air was cold on her wet skin and she felt her breasts tighten and grow heavy as her eyes lingered on the mass of curling black hair covering his chest and disappearing in a damp line down across his navel to the top of his brief trunks. She pulled the soft towelling robe more closely round her, slipping her arms into its concealing folds and pulling the belt tightly round her waist.

'Cold?' He had noticed her movements without guessing the real reason for them, for which she was supremely grateful.

'Not really, it's too warm to be cold, although a hot shower would be nice. The salt is making my hair feel sticky.'

'Take as long as you like.' They had reached the house now and he leant across her to open the doors, brushing her face fleetingly against the hairy hardness of his chest. 'You will find plenty of shampoo and lotions in the bathroom attached to the bedroom where your clothes are. I should imagine there will be something to suit. Sandy and Mitch are used to entertaining on a vast scale and I have yet to find anything that cannot be had in this establishment.' His grey eyes rested for a moment on the thick silver hair clinging in damp tendrils round her slim white neck, and she felt heat where his gaze touched. There was a brooding, restless quality in the dark face that she couldn't quite fathom, but she began to understand the skittish unease of the wildebeest when being surveyed by the hard hunting eyes of the big cats.

They walked through the sitting-room and Aline's step faltered as they neared the staircase, but he stopped and gestured for her to precede him up the stairs. 'Ladies first.' It felt like the hardest thing she had ever done to walk in front of him. She could almost feel the heat of his body, and the compelling intimacy of the moment had her breath coming in short bursts and her legs beginning to tremble. What if he touched her? She gave herself a mental slap. Stop it, Aline, she told herself firmly. Concentrate on getting to that room.

'I'll be downstairs when you're ready. Steak and salad all right?' His voice was smooth and casual, with a low mocking throb in its depth which told her he was playing with her again, like a cat before the kill.

'Thank you.' She nodded as she spoke without turning round, stepping swiftly through the open doorway of her room as she came level with it and shutting the door quickly with a firm click. She leant against it, panting as though she had been running a race, the blood pounding in her ears. She had been crazy to come here alone like this. It was just *asking* for trouble.

She began to relax as the hot water in the shower stung into her flesh, washing away the last clinging remnants of salt and sand and cascading in a warm flood over her tense body. She stood under the water for minutes, turning this way and that as tight muscles began to ease and she regained her composure. It would be all right— she would just eat her meal and ask him to take her home. Simple as that.

The delicately perfumed shampoo she found in the bathroom cupboard was specially for blondes and turned her hair into sleek velvet, and when she found a body lotion with the same expensive scent she smoothed a liberal amount into her skin, with a feeling of well-being replacing the earlier panic.

Once dressed, she finished drying her hair, pulling it up into a small high knot without one loose tendril softening the severe line and securing it with two large clips. There must be no suggestion of seduction tonight, she thought wearily as she resisted the impulse to apply a little make-up to the pale face staring back at her from the ornate oval mirror.

She followed the sound of his cheerful whistling as she made her way downstairs and found him in the kitchen expertly tossing a crisp salad, an open bottle of white wine by his side and two full glasses in front of him. 'Just in time.' She found the smile he gave her disturbing: its warmth hinted at an intimacy that wasn't theirs. 'Sit down and watch me work.'

'Can I help?'

'No.' He passed her a glass of wine as he spoke and then checked the thick steaks sizzling enticingly under a low grill, raising a cynical eyebrow to her untouched glass as he resumed work. 'Not thirsty?' His eyes gleamed with sardonic mockery as they swept over her bare face and severe hairstyle, and she smiled swiftly, determined to remain calm.

'I ought to eat first.' She sat gingerly on the high padded stool he had indicated and took a small sip of the chilled wine. It was delicious, but then it would be. He had chosen it.

'First?' His gaze was wicked as it fastened on her pink cheeks.

'You know what I mean,' she snapped quickly. 'Before I have any alcohol on an empty stomach.'

'Don't you ever relax?' She looked at him, momentarily disconcerted by the seriousness that had replaced the teasing. 'Or is it just with me that you display such aggressiveness? There are times when you remind me of a wild little Persian kitten, all soft silver fur but with

sharp little claws ready to tear at the slightest provo-
cation. You bristle so easily, Aline.'

'Do I?' She wasn't offended; the calm voice had
sounded almost concerned. 'Well, it must be you; I'm
normally quite laid-back.'

'We do tend to strike sparks off each other, don't we?'
The deep voice was quietly quizzical. 'Why do you
suppose that is? Believe it or not, I meant what I said
that first night here. I did want us to work together ami-
cably with the past forgotten, but somehow... I don't
know. You always manage to get under my skin.'

'I do?'

'You do,' he agreed mockingly. 'Like tonight, when
you came downstairs looking scared to death and with
your hair pulled back so tightly that I'm sure your scalp
must be pleading for mercy. I'm sorry, Aline, you can't
hide your beauty like that.'

'I didn't——'

He cut her protest short by leaning across the table,
and the next moment her hair tumbled loose from its
confines in a swirl of shining silver.

'Oh!' She raised a surprised hand to her head and he
grinned disarmingly, suddenly looking ten years younger
as he threw the clips on to the table abruptly.

'There's nowhere to hide, and I prefer your hair loose.'

'Hide?' She tried to keep her voice cool but failed
miserably. 'I don't know what you mean.'

'Forgive me,' he drawled mockingly, his hard grey gaze
sweeping over her flushed cheeks with keen scrutiny. 'I
thought the schoolmarm hairdo and scrubbed appearance were meant to dull my appetite.'

'I don't know what you're talking about,' she lied
crossly, all but finishing her glass of wine in her agi-
tation. He leant across silently and refilled her glass
without taking his eyes off her face.

'You're a mystery, little dove, but one I'm determined to solve.' She couldn't reply; her voice was locked in her throat. 'There are so many things about you that just don't add up, and mathematics always was my strong point at school. I don't intend to let this particular problem get the better of me.'

'There's no problem,' she said weakly, and he shot her a penetrating glance as he leaned back in his seat, his eyes moving over her hair and skin in slow pleasure.

'Oh, yes, there is,' he declared deliberately, 'a far bigger one than you could begin to guess at right now. I don't know yet quite how I'm going to tackle it, but I'm working on it.'

He looked at her intently for one long, enigmatic moment and then she was infinitely relieved when he turned away to attend to the steaks again. This was going to be even worse than she had expected; he seemed to deem her capable of all sorts of devious motives and schemes. Why couldn't he just leave her alone? She was working for him, wasn't she, falling in with all he had asked of her? What was it that seemed to be driving him to break her completely? She knew with a sudden flash of searing intuition that he had made up his mind that he wouldn't be content until she was crushed and broken at his feet, and at the same instant her heart made her face the fact she had been avoiding for days: that she loved him.

She groaned silently and took a long drink of the wine. She couldn't fool herself any more that it was just physical attraction or animal desire; she loved him, *loved* him. She brushed the hair from her face with a hand that shook. She would have to be doubly careful now, for if he even caught a hint of how she felt he would have the weapon he was seeking to destroy her utterly, and in his fierce Corsican desire for revenge he would have no hesitation in doing just that.

CHAPTER FIVE

ALINE ate without tasting the meal, but it calmed her jangled nerves and cleared her head a little of the muzziness the wine had produced, although with every mouthful she was painfully conscious of the big dark figure draped opposite her across the small table. She had chosen to eat in the large kitchen, thinking it less intimate, but after they had finished he rose and took her arm, drawing her upwards.

'Go and sit down in the sitting-room. I've lit the fire and we'll have coffee in comfort. These stools are OK for a while but you need the skin of a rhinoceros to stand them for more than a few minutes.'

There was nothing she could say and so she stood hesitating in the doorway as he switched the percolator on to brew, his movements cool and controlled as always. For such a big man he seemed to have a lithe fluidity that strengthened the overall impression of a dangerous wild animal on a short leash, and Aline bit her lower lip nervously as she watched him.

'Come on.' He took her hand again and she kept her eyes on the floor. 'You don't need me to show you the way, surely?' His voice was lightly teasing but she couldn't match his mood as he led her through to the sitting-room. Her eyes flickered to the small two-seater settee in front of the crackling logs; she didn't remember its being there earlier. She glanced up and caught the dark mockery lighting his face. He knew exactly what she was thinking.

'Aren't you going to sit down?' he asked quietly, and when she didn't reply he laughed softly. 'You know, you always make me feel like some sort of caveman from the Dark Ages. It's as though you expect me to leap on you at any opportunity and take you by force. Now, why do you think that is?'

'I don't know,' she answered sharply as her heart hammered against her ribs. 'I'm not responsible for your sexual fantasies.'

'You are, you know.' He raised his hand slowly and gently stroked her hot cheek in a soft caress. His finger moved to outline her lips and she willed herself to stand perfectly still, although every nerve and muscle in her quivering body was crying out for release. 'You're one of the most beautiful women I've ever seen.'

'Am I?' She was past rational thought. The touch of his hand on her flesh was doing crazy things to her body, and panic had her in a terrifying grip.

'You know you are. Even without any make-up and with your hair pulled back in that ridiculous bun, you are dynamite, but when it's loose, like now . . .' He lifted one silky strand that had formed itself into a loose ringlet. 'You're sensational.' He drew her closer to him and she could see the fine dark chest hair where his shirt was undone. 'Do you deliver, Aline? Or is it all just a game with you?'

'I don't know what you mean.' She was stammering as the clean, warm, male smell of him filled her nostrils, a subtle mixture of sun, sea and expensive aftershave. His wandering hands moved gently across her back in a soft coaxing rhythm that was not threatening, and she felt her legs turn to jelly.

'I thought you were getting coffee?' She had meant her words to sound cool and light, but they emerged as a shaking, breathless plea.

He shot her one deep, discerning glance and then she was free. 'The lady wants coffee, the lady shall have coffee,' he said lightly. 'Just don't disappear before I get back.' She sank down on to the settee as he left, glad of the warmth from the blazing logs on her cold limbs. She mustn't let him affect her like this—it was madness. She had to master this love for him before it mastered her.

He was back within minutes, holding a large tray. 'Cream and sugar?' She nodded and he smiled briefly. 'I thought you would be a cream and sugar girl.' He handed her a cup of steaming liquid carefully and then poured a black coffee for himself. 'You can only really get a decent cup of coffee in Corsica,' he said conversationally as he put the tray to one side. 'It's served in tiny glasses and is as thick as treacle, but with an unsurpassable taste.'

She waited with bated breath for him to sit by her side, but instead he stretched out on to the thick rug at her feet, his black head resting against her legs. It did something electrifying to her insides and she gulped in her throat. They sat quietly, without speaking, as the firelight played its grotesque flickering dance, casting waving shadows over the darkened room, the only illumination from the leaping orange-red flames. She realised that he had stage-managed the cosy, intimate atmosphere, but it still didn't dispel the grinding nervous excitement that had her in its grip, and as she finished her coffee she steeled herself to voice her request to be taken home.

'You've got quite a way with you, Miss Marcell.' His deep voice made her jump and she hoped he hadn't noticed. 'It can creep up on a man when he isn't looking.'

She looked at the back of his head in surprise and schooled her voice to be light and calm. 'I don't think anything or anyone could take you by surprise.'

He turned as she spoke and there was an amused light in the hard grey eyes and a faintly rueful expression pulling at the firm lips. 'You see me as a kind of Superman?' He laughed softly. 'Well, well.'

'Not a Superman,' she protested, stung by his mockery. 'Just——' She stopped suddenly. It was probably prudent not to continue.

'Just?' His smile had vanished, to be replaced by cold enquiry. 'Let's have it.'

'Please, Cord, it's getting late. It was a lovely meal but I really ought to go now.' His face hardened into the determined expression she knew so well. After working so closely with him over the last few weeks she recognised that evasiveness was useless.

'I've been quite generous in making known my opinion of you.' His voice dripped sarcasm. 'It's your turn now.'

'I'd rather leave it.' She hated herself for trying to mollify him but she had the distinct feeling she would come off worse in any duel with words. 'Some things are best left unsaid.'

'Really?' He moved abruptly so that he was kneeling in front of her, his head just above hers and his narrowed eyes glittering coldly. 'Let's do away with words and try the age-old method of communication, then. That never fails.'

Before she could speak he had pulled her on to the rug by his side, leaning across her with one swift dominating movement so that his hard body was pressed down the length of hers. She couldn't even struggle; his superior weight and strength had her helpless beneath him. His cruel face was an inch or so away and he remained quite still, his eyes locked with hers and a small muscle jerking in his tanned cheek.

'Ready to talk?' Any reply she might have made was lost as his mouth covered hers in an amazingly tantalising exploratory kiss that made no demands but claimed something from her which she longed to give. She had expected him to be savage, and the unexpected tenderness was her undoing.

As the kiss deepened he lifted himself slightly so that her arms were free, and almost against her will they crept up, to wind round his neck in silent surrender. His lips moved over her face like fire, travelling over her closed eyelids and teasing her earlobes before moving down to her exposed throat, where a small, violent pulse was beating rapidly. 'Your skin is like warm silk.' His voice was hoarse and low, and as she felt the long, lean body moulded against hers like a second skin she recognised the thrust of his desire with a small thrill of combined triumph and fear. He wanted her, badly. At least that much was certain.

'I want you, Aline.' It was as though he was voicing her thoughts. 'I haven't wanted anyone so much in a long time...' His hands moved tenderly down her body, provoking tiny nerves she never knew she had to fire into glorious life. For the first time she began to understand what it was to be fully awakened, and he didn't rush her, taking her along at her own pace, modulating his fierce desire to match her growing passion. Her breath was coming in tiny gasping sobs against his face as the male smell and strength of him encompassed her, and she felt the sensual power that was at the very essence of him reach out and persuade her into submission.

'Stay here with me tonight. Let me really make love to you.'

It was the phrase 'make love to you' that snapped her back from the edge of complete capitulation. He hadn't said 'love you'; he wasn't pretending that she meant anything to him beyond a night of sexual fulfilment—he never had.

She reared up like a frightened faun, taking him completely by surprise. 'Aline?' He sat back on his heels as she struggled wildly to her feet, panic-stricken at the dangerous power this man commanded. She had to stop this; it was wrong, so wrong. 'Aline, what is it?' He reached out to touch her, his face concerned, but she sprang back as though he would burn her.

'Don't touch me!' Her voice was harsh and frightened and her eyes were huge in the pale expanse of her face. 'Just keep away.'

The concerned expression vanished, to be replaced by cold contempt. 'No dramatics, please.' His voice was icy. 'I wasn't exactly having to hold you down, was I?'

Sick and humiliated, she stared at him as hot rage began to course through her shaking limbs, steadying her trembling legs and giving strength to her voice. 'You really are a swine, aren't you, a first-class swine?' she spat at him, her face drained of colour.

'Now just you hold on a doggone minute!' He sprang to his feet in one violent bound and stood towering over her, hot anger turning his dark face into a devil's mask. 'Now I don't know what you're playing at, but don't you try and tell me you weren't enjoying our little tête-à-tête there, because it won't wash. That was my body next to yours, and the signals were coming hot and strong.'

'You disgust me!' She hissed the words into his face as crushing self-contempt and shock had her searching for a way to hurt him as he was hurting her. 'Men like you make me sick. You want one thing and one thing only.'

'And I don't doubt for a minute that you are an authority on men of all different shapes and sizes,' he said bitterly. 'You play it for all it's worth, don't you? You almost had me believing—— Oh, what's the point?' He was white with rage as he glared at her.

'That was all part of my punishment, wasn't it?' She waved her hand wildly in the direction of the rug. 'How could you do something like that in cold blood?'

'I don't believe this.' His voice was a mixture of horrified incredulity and black rage, made all the more sinister as it dropped to just above a whisper. 'I've heard my lovemaking described in many varied terms, but never as a punishment. What exactly do you think I am? Some sort of perverted sadist?' She took a step backwards as he moved towards her. 'And just who do you think you are anyway? I was taking what was on offer, what has been on offer for weeks. Don't blame me if I called your bluff; I told you before, I'm too old to play games. Save those for young fools like Simon but don't try them with me.'

'That's not true and you know it!' She was shouting now. 'None of what you've said is true. You've twisted it all again.'

'Again?' His voice was still low with a strange cold control that only fuelled her anger. His eyes narrowed into cruel grey slits as he stared at her insultingly. 'This is the bit where you tell me you wouldn't dream of taking a penny that didn't belong to you, right? You're just a poor misunderstood working girl and as pure as the driven snow! Well, save it for the other poor jerks who get mixed up with you. You're mad at me because I can read you like a book and I don't like what's written on the pages. I don't know how many men you have had and I don't care, but one thing I will promise you: I wouldn't touch you with a bargepole.'

His lips had drawn back from his teeth in a scorching sneer and she stared at him wordlessly, her anger evaporating in the face of such malevolence. What had she said or done to inspire such hatred?

With a small strangled sob she took a step backwards without taking her eyes from his face, and as he remained rigid, as though carved in stone, she turned and ran to the french windows, pulling them open and falling into the sloping garden as tears ran in a hot blinding flood down her white face. He was a monster, an inhuman monster!

She stumbled down the lawn and on to the deserted beach, running until the lights from the house faded into the distance and the only sound was her harsh panting and the faint swishing of the tiny, foam-crested waves making their rhythmic journey up the white sand.

The black sky was studded with hundreds of bright twinkling stars like minute diamonds on dark velvet, but she was blind and deaf to the natural beauty around her, her mind vibrating as his words rang with painful clarity over and over again in her aching head. It had seemed as though he loathed her, and it had to be more than the loss of the money that inspired such hatred. She sank down on to the warm soft sand as her legs finally gave way, her thoughts in a chaotic turmoil. Where could she go? There was nowhere to run, and even if she found a means of escape she couldn't hide from herself and the knowledge of her love for him. She groaned and curled herself into a tight little ball, seeking comfort that wasn't there.

'Oh, Mum...' For the first time in years she felt her mother's loss as acutely as the first terrible moments when she had learnt of her parents' death. She was in the principal's office again, white-faced and shaking, Tim by her side, and the pain was as raw and fresh as it had been then.

Her body heaved in unbearable anguish and she pounded the soft sand with clenched fists until her wet face was covered in tiny white granules and her mind was dull with exhaustion.

Slowly she began to relax as the soft, steady drumming of the sea numbed her bruised spirit and lifted her to a plane where nothing was real except the cool powdery substance under her face and the light stroking of the sea breeze as it lifted her hair in a gentle caress. The last thing she remembered before falling asleep was that she would have to go back for her bag before she left, which would mean seeing him—and that was something she never wanted to do again, ever.

'Where the hell have you been? I've scoured the whole of this beach for you! Didn't your mother ever tell you you shouldn't be out alone in the dark?' The angrily mocking voice brought her abruptly out of a deep, dreamless sleep but for a moment she was powerless to raise herself or respond, and the next instant Cord had dropped down on to the sand beside her, his dark face suddenly drained of colour. 'Aline? Talk to me. Are you all right? What's happened?'

'My head hurts.' She struggled to sit up and his arms went round her, drawing her against his hard chest.

'You gave me one hell of a fright,' he said tensely. 'Do you realise you've been gone over two hours? Have you hurt yourself?'

'No, I think I must have fallen asleep.' She raised dazed eyes to his anxious face. 'I'm sorry, Cord, I didn't mean to——'

'You never *do* mean to!' He cut her stumbling voice short abruptly and muttered a smothered oath as his fingers traced the dried tears on her face. 'You look like a little lost mermaid the sea has washed up.' His voice was curiously flat, and she tried to see the expression on his face as a cloud obscured the moon's bright light for a moment. He stood up slowly. 'Come on, you feel chilled to the bone.'

As he helped her up she swayed slightly on legs that were cramped and stiff, and before she realised what he was doing he had lifted her into his arms as easily as though she were a small child. 'Don't, please don't.' Her voice was weak and she felt close to tears as he cast an exasperated glance at her pale upturned face.

'Shut up, Aline. Just shut up.' He sounded as though he was at the end of his tether and she leaned back limply against his broad chest as he started walking towards the house. She was too weary and heartsore to argue, and it was wonderfully comforting to be held close to his strong, hard body, his warmth relaxing her chilled limbs and his heartbeat loud and reassuring against her sticky cheek.

She hadn't realised how far she had travelled from the house, but as he walked back along the smooth sand she saw with dismay that it must have been at least half a mile. 'I can walk now.' The house was a hundred yards away and she was beginning to feel hotly embarrassed at the scene she had caused.

'I am not setting you down until we are inside,' he said grimly without checking his stride. 'If you bolt again I shan't be responsible for my actions next time I find you.' He glanced down at her wide tearful eyes and her hair spread out over his arm like unfurling spun silk, and swore softly in his native language. 'And for crying out loud, stop looking at me like that. I can only take so much, Aline, and I think my limit was reached over an hour ago.'

She said no more, lowering her head and shutting her eyes as she snuggled back into the warmth of his chest. She felt his hard muscles tense beneath her body and then he sighed deeply, his grey eyes rueful. 'Perhaps you'd be safer walking after all.' His voice was full of dry self-mockery as he set her down at the bottom of the slope that led up to the house. 'I don't think my control is a hundred per cent at this moment in time.'

'What?' She swallowed nervously as she spoke. What had she done wrong now?

He looked at her very intently as she stood, slender and waif-like, and shook his dark head gently in wry disbelief. 'You can't be for real, you really can't. Don't you know what you do to a man? I'm only human, whatever you may think to the contrary, and right now I'd like to lay you down out here on the sand and make love to you till morning.' He looked grimly at her wide eyes. 'Now, that may not be what you want to hear in view of the circumstances, but it's a fact, so if your re-action is what I think it will be, will you please start walking?'

She opened her mouth to speak, looked at his face as he stared silently down at her, closed it again and started walking on legs that could barely hold her.

'Drink this.' She was sitting in bed in her original room after a long, scalding bath, feeling warm from the top of her head to the soles of her feet, swaddled in an enormous fluffy jumper she had found laid out across the pillow for her when she had emerged from the bathroom. She stared bemusedly into Cord's tight face as he pushed the mug of warm milk liberally laced with whisky into her outstretched hand.

'I don't want it. I don't like whisky.'

He shut his eyes briefly and swore quietly. 'You would test the patience of a saint, my little dove, and, as we both know, I'm no saint. I'm not asking you to drink it, I'm *telling* you. You were half frozen when I found you on that beach tonight and I don't want you down with a chill or worse. Now please, for both our sakes, just do as you are told for once and finish the drink.'

'All right.' She drained the mug as he watched. 'I'm sorry, Cord.'

He groaned softly as he looked at her, flushed and warm, her hair falling over her shoulders in tumbled blonde curls and her brown eyes full of apology.

'You're so darn moreish...' He dropped a light kiss on her half-open lips, but as his mouth fused with hers a shudder ran through him which she felt in her own body. 'I think I'd better get out of here right now.'

He was gone before she could reply, the door shutting with a determined bang that spoke of his inner turmoil as clearly as his hungry eyes had done. If only it were more than physical desire that was attracting him. If only—— She shut the door firmly on the path her mind was taking. It was no good thinking like that. His opinion of her couldn't be any lower, as he had made painfully clear tonight, and it was as far removed from love as it was possible to be. She would survive this; other people came through much worse.

She snuggled down under the covers with a small sigh, expecting to lie awake for hours reviewing the dismal failure of the evening, but when she next opened her eyes it was early morning and a shaft of bright golden sunlight was falling straight on to her sleepy face.

She turned over drowsily, momentarily at a loss as to where she was, but then, as memory returned in a hot, humiliating flood, she sat up suddenly with a small ex-

clamation of horror. Let it all be a dream, a horrible,
embarrassing dream! But as she glanced round the
luxurious bedroom she knew it wasn't. How could she
have made such a fool of herself? She could have ex-
tricated herself from the situation without making such
a fuss; he was used to sophisticated mature women who
would be able to turn refusal into a compliment. Not,
she was sure, that he had to cope with that eventuality
very often, if all the rumours about him were true. She
groaned softly. She had behaved like a schoolgirl on her
first date. Whatever was he thinking about her this
morning? 'Why did you have to bring me here last night,
Cord Lachoni?' she whispered miserably into the silent
room. 'If you wanted to prove I'm no match for you,
you certainly succeeded beyond your wildest
expectations.'

She glanced at her watch and saw the small gold face
telling her it was six o'clock. She climbed out of bed
and padded across to the large patio doors that opened
on to a long narrow balcony running the length of the
room. Pulling back the heavy velvet curtains, she saw a
small table and chairs warming in the sun, and as she
stepped on to the tiled floor the shiny surface was hot
on the soles of her bare feet.

It was going to be another beautiful day. The fresh
light-washed sky was a vivid shade of blue and the air
was clear and clean on her face. At the bottom of the
sleeping garden the sand was a pale gold carpet on to
which the sea lapped invitingly, and for a moment she
was tempted to take an early-morning swim, but then
the memory of a pair of hard grey eyes swam into her
mind and she reluctantly abandoned the idea. This was
a working day, after all, and she had better get ready.

After a warm shower she dressed quickly and crept
quietly downstairs, making for the kitchen. A cup of

Free Books and Gifts claim

Yes Please send me my 4 FREE Temptation romances together with my FREE gifts. Please also reserve a special Reader Service subscription for me. If I decide to subscribe, I will receive 4 superb new Temptations for just £7.00 every month, post and packing FREE. If I decide not to subscribe I shall write to you within 10 days. The FREE books and gifts will be mine to keep. I understand that I am under no obligation whatsoever. I may cancel or suspend my subscription at any time simply by writing to you. I am over 18 years of age.

1A3T

Name _____

Address _____

_____ Postcode _____

Signature _____

Mills & Boon Reader Service
FREEPOST
P.O. Box 236
Croydon
CR9 9EL

Send NO money now

NO STAMP NEEDED

coffee would give her the courage she needed to look into that dark, mocking face. She could imagine he wasn't going to let her forget last night in a hurry.

The big modern kitchen was deserted, and after making some coffee she poured herself a cup and then sat on a stool close to the window, enjoying the warm sunlight as she looked out over the peaceful view, the scents of summer streaming in through the open window.

'It's a good way to start the day.' She jumped so violently as the familiar deep voice sounded right in her ear that she blessed the fact that she had just drained her cup. Cord was standing just behind her, staring down at her blonde head, his grey eyes keen and watchful.

'Good morning.' She tried to keep her voice steady but a faint tremor crept through and she could feel hot colour staining her cheeks. He looked so...good. His jet-black hair was still damp from the shower and slicked back from his forehead and he was carrying his jacket over one arm, his snowy white shirt unbuttoned at the neck and his tie hanging round his neck ready to knot into position before they left. What would it be like to wake up beside him every morning and——? She forced her mind into less titillating channels.

'Would you like me to cook breakfast?' She smiled nervously as she spoke, and his face was sombre as he considered her for a moment before replying.

'I would love it.' There was a timbre to his voice that made the flush deepen. 'You'll find something of everything in the fridge.'

She had hoped he would disappear behind a newspaper or find something to do while she prepared the food, but he seated himself at the kitchen table, his long legs stretched out in relaxed laziness, and leaned back in his chair with his hands behind his head, watching her every move.

'Do you have to do that?' she asked irritably after a few minutes when the second egg had broken in the pan. He was making her all fingers and thumbs.

'What?' He looked at her in genuine surprise.

'Watch me all the time. It's most unsettling.'

'Sorry.' The hard mouth was touched with a small smile as he spoke. 'It's just that I've often thought over the last few weeks how it would be if you were here, making breakfast. Needless to say, I had anticipated the night before as ending somewhat differently.'

'I don't doubt it,' she returned drily, glad the matter had been brought out into the open. 'Sorry I couldn't oblige.'

'Not half as sorry as I am.' Amazingly there was no mockery or censure in his voice, and his eyes were surprisingly gentle as they looked into hers. 'You really are the most delicious female.'

'Well, here is the most delicious breakfast.'

'Spoil-sport. You always change the conversation when it is getting interesting.' As he took the plate from her he smiled again, and she turned back for her own plate with a straight face, a feeling of panic ruining her appetite. This was too cosy and she loved him too much. The sooner they were out of here the better.

It was just gone nine when they finally left the house after Cord had received two long-distance telephone calls, one from his offices in America and one from England. She knew he hadn't arranged for the delay, but for the first time she was experiencing a feeling of disquiet at the thought of walking into the office late with Cord at her side. It suddenly occurred to her that most people would put two and two together and make five. She glanced at Cord's profile when he swung the long, low car out of the drive, but the cold face was expressionless as he concentrated on the road ahead.

'You like the house, then?' His deep, cool voice broke into her spinning thoughts and she turned to him distractedly.

'Sorry?'

'The house,' he said patiently. 'Do you like it?'

'It's absolutely beautiful. No one could fail to like it.'

'I've got the chance of buying it if I want it,' he said laconically. 'Mitch phoned me a couple of days ago to say Sandy doesn't want to come back here. Unhappy memories and so on. He's giving me first refusal before he puts it on the open market.'

'What will you do?' She glanced at him curiously. 'Can you afford it?'

He smiled in amused indulgence. 'I think I could just about scrape the money together,' he said drily, and she realised as he spoke that it had been a stupid question. Since working for him she had become aware of a few of his assets, and he could afford the house and probably several like it.

'If I had the chance of buying a place like that I wouldn't hesitate,' she said longingly. 'It's a dream house.'

'Ah, but then I'm not you. If you did hesitate a little more before diving headlong into some situations, you wouldn't be in this mess now, would you? And I'd still be fifty thousand pounds better off.' The superior tone made her want to bite back, but she knew from experience that she couldn't win, and so she contented herself with a scathing glance and a flounce round in her seat, keeping her back half turned towards him as she looked out of the window.

She hadn't been able to see much of the countryside the night before in the dark, but now she found it enchanting. They passed through several tiny hamlets, and even the smallest village had a crumbling medieval church at the side of a sparkling river, with tall poplars lining the road like soldiers on parade. She caught a glimpse of the odd grand château in the distance, surrounded by high stone walls and big wrought-iron gates, slumbering majestically in the autumn sunshine.

France was such a country of contrasts, from elegant country houses to stone-built farmhouses within a few yards of each other, with horses working the fields and cows being milked by fresh-cheeked women by the roadside as chickens scratched contentedly near by. The grass verges were thickly studded with a stunning variety of wild flowers, and she could almost believe she had been transported back in time as she noticed lettuces and cabbages growing between lupins and gladioli in the pretty little cottage gardens.

This was rural France at its best, and Aline longed to explore further instead of having to face the inquisitive glances and whispered comments she was sure would be waiting for her at the office.

As the car nosed into the parking space reserved for Cord twenty minutes later she could already see some interested faces at the windows, and she bit her bottom lip tightly as Cord opened her door.

'It would probably have been wiser if I had come in a little later.' She spoke her thoughts out loud but he was lifting a pile of files from the boot of the car and didn't hear her.

'Take my briefcase, Aline, would you?' He had moved to the front of the car again, and indicated the black leather case on the back seat. 'It isn't heavy.'

She reached into the back and retrieved the case, locking the car with the keys he had left in the ignition. Brilliant, absolutely brilliant! She was going to have to walk in carrying his briefcase too. A big sign tattooed across her forehead stating 'I spent the night with this man' couldn't have been more obvious.

'Come on, stop dithering.' He sounded irritable. The calm, relaxed man of an hour ago had vanished and in his place was the cold, ruthless businessman she knew so well, who expected everyone to jump the moment he snapped his fingers. She followed him into the building with a sinking heart. There was nothing she could do; she would just have to put a brave face on things. She should have had the foresight to prevent this situation from happening. She was even wearing the same clothes as yesterday!

'Mark, are those figures I asked for yesterday on my desk?' Cord paused on his way through the main office to speak to one of the junior accountants, forcing her to stand passively behind him. She kept her eyes on his broad back.

'Susan, did we get that report from Loincards in the post as they promised?' They had stopped again, Cord with his armful of files and Aline clutching his briefcase as he listened to what the girl replied. He was doing this on purpose, she was sure of it! Aline noticed that no one raised their head as normal to wish her good morning and she suspected it was because they were embarrassed and unsure of her reaction. Why couldn't he have just marched through to his room as usual? she thought furiously as her cheeks turned pinker and pinker and the impulse to hit him over the head with the inoffensive briefcase grew sweeter by the second.

'Cord, darling...' As Aline opened the door to their rooms and stood back for Cord to precede her with the files she felt her heart sink even further. Claudia was sitting coiled elegantly in one of the big easy chairs, her sharp pale eyes flashing between them and her painted red mouth forced into a small smile. 'Where on earth have you been? Daddy tried to phone you late last night but there was no answer.' Claudia's low throaty voice had clearly carried into the outer office; several heads bent busily at their desks risked a quick sidelong glance.

'I was home all evening.' Cord obviously disliked being asked to account for his whereabouts, and his face was grim as he walked into his room without checking his stride.

'But Cord, darling, Daddy said——' What Daddy said was cut off as Cord slammed the door shut with his foot after Claudia had followed him in.

Aline hung up her jacket with shaking hands. The swift glance that Claudia had thrown at her as she followed him into his room had been one of pure evil. She couldn't hear what transpired between them but it was only a few moments later when Claudia emerged from the inner room, her beautiful face scarlet with anger and her mouth set in a tight, unattractive line. She walked straight past Aline without looking to right or left and wrenched open the door into the main office, her high heels tapping spitefully on the tiled floor as she made her way out of the building.

Great! Aline closed her eyes for a second. This was going to be a wonderful day; she could feel her nerves screaming already. She just hoped Cord hadn't mentioned her name in anything he had said to Claudia. That hope died a few seconds later as he barked her name from his room.

'Yes?' She poked her head round the open door nervously.

'Come in and shut the door.' The hard grinding voice didn't bode well for office harmony. 'That——' he flicked his hand angrily towards the door Claudia had left from '—you ignore. Right?'

'Right.' She looked at him warily.

'Any problems in that area you refer to me.'

'Problems?' She tried to keep her voice neutral. 'Why should there be any problems?'

'That doesn't matter.' His cool eyes raked her face. 'Sufficient to say, Claudia and I *were* friendly a few years ago but all that has been over and done with for a long time. However, she seems to think she has the right to certain privileges and I have had to...persuade her otherwise. Got it?'

'Oh, I've got it all right.' She glared at him angrily. 'I suppose you told her I spent the night at your house?'

'I didn't have to.' His voice was cold. 'But you did, didn't you?'

'Not the way she thinks.' She could feel her voice rising and lowered it quickly. 'You know what she'll think now.'

'I am not responsible for what Claudia thinks and I pity any man who is.' His voice was biting and his eyes cut straight through her. 'Now, I am trying to run a business here, so will you get back to your desk and do some work?'

'Look——'

'I'm busy, Aline. I've too much to do this morning to let trivialities get in the way.'

'Trivialities!' She ground out the word through clenched teeth. 'Oh, you, you...' He ignored her totally, lowering his cold gaze to the papers on his desk and beginning to make some notes in the margin of a report, and after a moment she flounced back into her room, banging his door shut so hard that the ceiling shook.

The intercom on her desk buzzed immediately, and as she pressed the button his voice bit into the room. 'Any more of that sort of behaviour and I'll turn you across my knee and treat you like the child you seem to have become. Understand?' She flicked down the switch without answering and it buzzed again at once. 'Do you understand me, Aline?'

'Yes.' She made a face at the machine as she answered.

'I don't know what's got into you this morning but I won't tolerate it. You are here specifically to do a job and you will do it properly at all times or suffer the consequences. Now get to work.'

That was that, then. They were right back to stage one of the war, as though last night had never happened. 'Right, Cord Lachoni,' she whispered quietly as she tidied her desk and settled down to translating an urgent document, 'if that's how you want it it's all right with me. I'll have my day with you if it's the last thing I ever do.'

CHAPTER SIX

THE rest of the day degenerated still further, and as Aline's temper died she grew more and more exhausted, counting the minutes until she could go home. Right, that's the last of it, she thought to herself as she checked her written notes against the typewritten French documents. She nerved herself to take them into Cord. He hadn't emerged from his office all day, requesting sandwiches and a coffee at midday but otherwise totally ignoring her existence. She had wandered down to the café on the corner with the others at lunchtime but conversation had been strained and they had obviously been watching every word they spoke. She flushed with remembered humiliation as she slipped on her jacket and tapped on his door.

'Yes?' He raised his dark head as she entered the room, his grey eyes distant and preoccupied.

'This is the last of it for today.' She put the papers on his desk quickly. 'I'm going home now.'

'Right. Hang on a few minutes and I'll give you a lift.'

'Huh.' She shrugged tightly. 'That would look good, wouldn't it?'

'Look good?' He raised his black eyebrows enquiringly as his eyes narrowed. 'What on earth are you talking about now?'

'I'm talking about you, offering me a lift,' she snapped back sharply. The pressure of the day had fixed itself in a dull ache behind her eyes.

'I offered you a lift because you look shattered,' he said coldly. 'Was that wrong?'

She shrugged again. '*I* think so.'

'OK, Aline, spit it out.' He settled back in his chair and crossed his arms as he spoke, his eyes dark granite and his mouth a thin straight line, and for a second she wished she had left well alone.

'Spit what out?' she prevaricated weakly.

'You know exactly what I mean, so cut out the fencing. You've been aching to pick a fight since this morning, so go ahead.'

'And I suppose you think I'm unreasonable? Just because you compromised me to the point where every person in that office assumes I'm your mistress, I'm supposed to accept all that in my stride, am I? It's all part of the deal!'

'I haven't the faintest idea what you are talking about,' he said grimly, his voice ominously quiet.

'I'm talking about your arranging to have me stay the night with you. Remember? You never did intend to take me home last night, did you? You had it all planned, the big seduction scene, right down to the last——'

'One more word, and so help me I'll put you across my knee!' He stood up as he spoke, uncoiling his big body from the chair in one swift, smooth movement, dark colour flaring under his high cheekbones and his grey eyes almost black with rage. His Corsican heritage had never been more obvious. 'I've had just about all I'm going to take from you for one day!'

She flinched as he strode round the desk to stand menacingly in front of her, his whole demeanour one of tightly controlled fury.

'If you would care to cast your mind back, it was you who ran out of my house like a startled rabbit and decided to take a hike in the middle of the night! I haven't been cast in such a ridiculously juvenile role since I was eighteen and the girl decided to walk home when the car broke down. What do you think I am, anyway? Some sex-mad adolescent intent on throwing himself on you at the first opportunity, regardless of your feelings in the matter? For crying out loud, woman, what's eating you?'

'There's nothing the matter with *me*!' He was doing it again! Turning it all round so that it was her fault.

'There is from where I'm standing,' he said coldly. 'For the record, I had every intention of taking you home last night once we had eaten. I have never begged for it in my life and I didn't intend to begin with you. What possible motive could I have for keeping you at my house all night?'

'To do exactly what you've accomplished and ruin my reputation.'

'Your reputation?' He stared at her for one incredulous second and threw back his head as peal after peal of cruelly insulting laughter burst from his throat. 'You're priceless, do you know that?' As his laughter died he looked at her white face with hard sardonic eyes, his nostrils flaring in distaste. 'What reputation is that? Refresh my memory. Is it the one of a liar, a thief, a cheat, or the new one of a cheap little tease? Take your pick—they all belong to you.'

'They do not.' She was holding on to the flood of tears that was threatening to break forth like grim death. She would not give him the satisfaction of reducing her to tears on top of everything else. 'Only in your twisted mind.'

'Oh, *I'm* the one with the twisted mind?' he asked in scathing mockery. 'I think it's time you took a long, hard look at yourself. I have never in my life taken anything or anyone that doesn't belong to me. Can you in all honesty say the same?'

'Yes, I can!' She shot back the answer without a moment's pause and he shook his head slightly as he walked slowly back to his desk.

'Well, you're consistent, I'll give you that.' She turned to leave but swung round again as he spoke, his voice coldly restrained as he seated himself at his desk, which was deep in paperwork. 'I shall expect you early in the morning.' He waved a hand at a pile of documents without looking up. 'There are some highly confidential letters that I want you to check and paraphrase for me and have ready by the time I come in, so you had better be here by seven. I'll leave all the relevant correspondence in the safe in this red file. You have a key?' She shook her head as he glanced up and he extracted a small thick key from his desk drawer. 'This is the spare; look after it, please.'

As she leant across to take the key from his large hand he dropped it from a few inches into her fingers as though the touch of her flesh would be repellent to him, and immediately buried himself in his work again without another word. The gesture hurt her more than all the harsh words that had gone before, but she gave no outward sign, merely closing his office door quietly and leaving as quickly as she could.

It was much later that night, as she lay curled up in a tight little ball in bed, that the hot tears came, but even after she had exhausted herself with weeping there was no release from the gnawing, aching pain that was tearing her apart. She lay for hours in the quiet darkness, her troubled mind darting back and forth, seeking a way of escape from this impossible situation, but after she had considered and reconsidered every possibility she was forced to accept that she was tied to him for another ten months. She ground her teeth in an agony of frustration. Ten months of watching him with Claudia, of being so near and yet so far!

After a few hours of broken sleep punctuated with tossing and turning until her bed felt as tangled as her mind, she rose wearily and padded into the bathroom while it was still dark. She usually made do with a quick shower each morning, but today she ran a long hot bath and used nearly half a bottle of bubbles until the water was thick and foamy and smelt heavenly. She spent almost an hour in the bathroom, manicuring her nails and washing her hair, determined to have every part of her as good as she could make it for the day ahead. She couldn't have explained what was driving her, but after the bath had relaxed and melted away the stiffness in her muscles she covered herself in expensive body lotion, and applied her make-up as carefully as if she were going to a ball instead of the office.

Pulling her robe round her loosely, she ate a light breakfast of fresh fruit and cereal, letting the warm breeze from the open window dry her hair into a silken curtain on her shoulders.

She was ready to leave the apartment block by half-past six and decided to make the short journey to work on foot. A brisk walk would get her to the office by seven and dispel the last of the cobwebs.

She was surprised to find herself humming as she walked along in the clean scented air, and marvelled wryly at the resilience of the human spirit, stopping briefly to gaze at a cloud of butterflies fluttering over the verges at the side of the road that were festooned with wild flowers. They came to land in a fenced garden underneath some apple trees heavy with fruit. As she came into the heart of the small town she stopped briefly at a café and bought rolls and fruit for her lunch, exchanging pleasantries with the few elderly locals sitting outside in the warm sunshine enjoying their breakfast of hot oven-fresh croissants and richly smelling coffee before continuing on her way.

'Good morning.' The deep, lazy voice brought her head swinging round. She had been deep in thought and hadn't noticed the long, sleek car crawling just behind her line of vision. 'I know it's only a few yards, but would you care to ride?' Cord's voice held a note of something she couldn't quite place; if she hadn't known it was impossible she would almost have suspected embarrassment.

'No, thank you. I prefer to walk,' she said quietly without slowing her steps; the unexpected sight of him had caused her heart to leap wildly and she was annoyed at the response of her traitorous body. Why couldn't she feel as cool towards him as he obviously did to her?

'I want to talk to you, Aline.' This time it was an order, and just for a second the desire to defy him and keep walking was strong, but with a small shrug she capitulated as the door swung open by her side. She slid gracefully into the sun-warmed seat and glanced at him quickly before keeping her eyes concentrated through the windscreen.

The collar of his shirt was open, his tie hanging round his neck, and it reminded her all too vividly of that intimate breakfast for two the day before, and in the close confines of the car she didn't want to remember things like that. His virile masculinity surrounded her immediately, destroying her ability to think clearly and doing crazy things to her equilibrium as she strove to shake off the power of his physical presence. This was ridiculous, she thought bitterly. He could sit there, relaxed and thoughtful with his big body darkly controlled, while she was a mass of jangling nerves. It just wasn't fair!

'I thought the idea was that I came in early *before* you and got the letters ready in time for your arrival?' She wished he would drive on, but the low, powerful car was purring quietly in neutral as he turned to look her fully in the face, one muscled arm resting on the back of her seat and the other leaning on the leather steering-wheel.

'I told you, I wanted to talk to you,' he said deliberately, his grey eyes forcing her to meet his tight gaze.

'Why? I should think we said all that could be said yesterday.' She sensed he was trying to break down the barrier but was frightened to meet him halfway. With cold hostility between them she could just about get through; anything else made her too vulnerable.

'You were wrong yesterday, but so was I,' he said slowly, ignoring her aggressiveness as though it were beneath his notice. 'You caught me on the raw with your ridiculous accusations; I was tired and I reacted badly. For some reason I didn't get much sleep the night before.' His voice was dry and his eyes gleamed with hidden laughter. 'Have you ever had a cold shower at two and three *and* four in the morning?'

She had to force the denial from her throat. 'No.'

'No, I guess not. Well, it was a first for me, too. But one thing I do want to make absolutely clear is that I did not take you to my house with the idea of keeping you there and putting you in a difficult position. The idea hadn't even occurred to me until you pointed it out yesterday. Perhaps it should have, on reflection.' It was the nearest thing to an apology she was going to get, she thought in amazed silence. 'I have never worked like that, and I was annoyed that you had attributed such . . . deviousness to me, I suppose.'

The ring of truth in his words was unmistakable and she found herself at a loss as to how to reply. The intimacy of the car was driving all rational thought from her head anyway. 'I see . . . I just thought——'

'Yes, I'm aware of what you thought.' The quizzical cynicism was more like him.

'Well, I'm sorry, then . . .'

His lips twitched with barely concealed amusement. 'What did I do when I took you on?' She looked up sharply; there had been a surprisingly tender note in his voice. 'You really are the most prickly little thing.' He idly lifted a lock of silky hair that was resting on her shoulders and let the shining silver run through his fingers to settle in sleek smoothness again. 'I don't want our working relationship to be affected by what happened yesterday.' He turned to place both hands on the wheel as though to restrain them and sat staring out into the road ahead. 'Do you understand me?'

She felt a sharp stab of pain at his words even as she berated herself for her stupidity. Her efficiency at work was all he had been concerned about. Just for a minute she had thought . . . 'Yes, of course I understand. We'll forget about it.' Her voice was stiff but she couldn't help it.

He gave a small sigh as he glanced at her tight face. 'Come on, Aline, no hard feelings?' She looked into his waiting face with veiled eyes, loving him, wanting him and hating him all at the same time.

'No hard feelings.' She forced a smile as she spoke and although he still didn't appear completely satisfied he slid the powerful car into gear after one more swift sharp look at her face and drew out into the traffic carefully.

The next few days passed in a blur of work that helped her bruised heart to heal a little. After her conversation with Cord that morning they had settled back into their precarious relationship as before, at least on the surface, though too much had been said for it really to be the same.

He was treating her with careful cool detachment at the moment, friendly and polite but definitely reserved. Claudia appeared very much back on the scene, which she supposed she should have expected, but which still hurt dreadfully. The other woman's tentacles were too tight and numerous for her to let go of Cord easily, although he seemed to react with barely concealed irritation each time she drifted unannounced into his rooms. Perhaps he liked to keep work and play distinctly separate, Aline mused miserably.

Claudia had taken to totally ignoring Aline now, looking through her as though she didn't exist with those large pale opaque eyes that caused a shiver to trickle down Aline's spine. The French girl repulsed her, although she couldn't have explained why. Her unusual beauty was fascinating but somehow macabre, like a tantalising illusion that could suddenly turn into grisly fact. Cord clearly didn't share her misgivings, however; she knew for a fact that he had visited the Asvanas' large country mansion almost every evening since her disastrous visit to his house. Claudia had made sure of that.

'Are you working tomorrow?' Wendy asked her late one Friday night as a crowd of the folk from the office sat drinking kir outside one of the small cafés on their route home. 'We're all going to the beach for the day and I thought you might like to come?' Her small face was hesitant; since that morning when Aline had arrived carrying Cord's briefcase the others had tended to treat her with more reserved wariness than friendship. Tonight was the first time she had joined them, and that was only due to Wendy's kindness.

'Thanks, I'd like to.' She had planned a relaxing day of doing nothing but felt if she refused this invitation she might not get asked again, and over the last few days she had grown increasingly lonely.

As it turned out, she enjoyed the following day immensely, dozing in the sun and swimming now and again as her honey-coloured skin turned a deeper shade of brown and her hair seemed to absorb the sun's brilliant rays and gleam with shimmering highlights. By the evening the others had totally accepted her as 'one of them'; when they decided to go out for a meal to round off the day there was no way she could have refused without alienating them again, and human contact was suddenly very precious.

It was just after nine when Aline entered the large busy restaurant in the middle of a big laughing crowd, with Simon on one arm and Wendy on the other. She was feeling tired but pleasantly relaxed after a day spent in the fresh air, and her white sleeveless dress and open-toed sandals showed off the newly acquired tan to perfection. Her silver-blonde hair floated round her smooth brown shoulders in a fine silken curtain, and there was more than one male head that craned to see more as she walked by.

The restaurant was renowned for its wonderful seafood and she was in the middle of the main course, a delicious and enormous platter full of big pink prawns and succulent crab, when the source of the strange unease she had felt ever since entering became apparent. A huge, broad-shouldered figure that towered over every other man present moved across from the other side of the room where he had been seated quietly watching the gay little party.

'Good evening.' Cord's voice was light and friendly as he glanced round the table at his smiling employees, but Aline felt the rapier-sharp glance cut through her for an instant and became uncomfortably aware of Simon's arm draped casually along the back of her seat. His other arm was in the same position on Wendy's seat, but she felt that might not have registered in the same way in that cold, suspicious brain.

He made polite conversation with them for a few minutes, including Aline generally without ever speaking or looking at her directly, and after buying everyone a drink made his way back to his table, where Claudia sat waiting like a beautiful patient spider. The fact that her father was also present didn't help Aline's wretchedness one iota. Claudia's face proclaimed triumph.

Aline wondered if she was the only one who had noticed how hard and brilliantly cruel Cord's eyes had been, set as though in rigid stone. She shivered slightly, her gaze drawn in spite of herself to that table in a shadowed corner.

He had been waiting for her glance and his smile was grim and filled with dark menace, and then his face became expressionless as he turned to Claudia in answer to something she had just said. She saw the French woman lift her hand to his square jaw and caress it lightly, her touch intimately possessive, and as her father said something she laughed provocatively, her red-tipped hands patting both their cheeks while her predatory eyes devoured Cord alive and then looked over mockingly at Aline.

'I'm going home.' She wasn't aware she had spoken in all the noise and frivolity at their table, but then Simon's warm hand touched hers gently and his eyes were soft and compassionate as they followed the path Aline's had been taking.

'Are you all right?'

She almost laughed hysterically in answer. Was she all right? She would never be all right again.

'Fine, thank you,' she answered mechanically. 'I've just got a headache and I think I'll call it a night. I can get a taxi home from here.' She swayed slightly as she rose, and Simon glanced at Wendy anxiously.

'OK if I just take Aline home? I'll be back in twenty minutes.'

'OK.' Wendy's voice was relaxed; she was clearly sure of herself where Simon was concerned. Even in the midst of her pain Aline was pleased; they were a nice couple.

A pair of glittering grey eyes watched Simon follow her out of the room, his hand on the small of her back, and then they were lost to view as the dark street swallowed them up into the night.

Aline had been asleep some time when the persistent knocking eventually pierced the deep mists of sleep. The room was in complete blackness and she glanced at her small alarm clock as she clicked the switch on the bedside lamp, trying to force her dazed mind into wakefulness.

'Just a minute.' She pulled a white towelling robe over the thin silk of her nightie and staggered sleepily to the door, sudden concern bringing her eyes wide open. What if the others had had an accident on the way home? There had been far too many of them crammed into the small car they had hired for the day, and they weren't used to driving in France.

'Yes, what——?' The words froze in her mouth as she took in the hard lean body leaning nonchalantly to one side of the doorway, the casualness of the stance belied by the fierce black anger turning the chiselled features into a dark devil's mask. Cord was angry; furiously, dangerously angry.

'Well, hello there, my little dove,' he drawled softly, his eyes flashing. 'I was wondering how long it would take you to answer the door. I didn't interrupt anything, did I?' His grey eyes flickered towards the open bedroom door and then back to her white face. 'Aren't you going to ask me in?'

'No.' She looked at him coldly. 'It's the middle of the night, in case you hadn't noticed.'

'Oh, I'd noticed all right!' As she went to shut the door he moved swiftly, wrenching the handle from her fingers and pushing the door aside so savagely that it shuddered on its hinges. 'In fact, I can tell you to the very minute how much time has elapsed since I saw you last.' He smiled a little crooked smile and she shrank back into the room as he entered, his eyes vicious.

'There's no need to be frightened, is there?' he said silkily as he kicked the door shut. 'Lover-boy will protect you. Where is he, by the way? Skulking in the wardrobe or comfortable in your bed?'

'What?' She stared at him uncomprehendingly.

'Simon. Dear, sweet simple Simon. Where is he? I'd just like a little word with him before I leave.' There was murder in his eyes.

'I haven't a clue what you're talking about. Simon hasn't been here tonight, or any night, for that matter.' She frowned as the import of his words began to register on her brain. 'You don't think——'

'I don't think what?' He strode over to the bedroom door, giving a quick cursory glance round the empty room before moving back in front of her, his body dropping the mantle of casualness and tightening like a rod. 'So he's already left, has he? How long did he stay?'

'I've had enough of this!' she said furiously, her eyes beginning to spit sparks like those of an angry cat. 'You have the cheek to come here and accuse me of sleeping with Simon when you and Claudia are common knowledge! You've got some nerve, Cord Lachoni.'

'Plenty,' he agreed in a low growl, 'but leave Claudia out of this. That was all finished with a long time ago.'

'I bet!' As his eyes narrowed she had the impression of a powerful wild animal on a short leash and for the first time she was really frightened. There was a dark cruelty in that glittering gaze that had never been there before, his eyes biting into her flesh as though he wanted to destroy her.

'Look, you've got this all wrong.' She suddenly realised he needed to hear the truth before things got out of hand. 'Simon just saw me home tonight, that's all. It was dark and he was worried about me going off alone in a taxi. I left him at the front of the building. End of story. Ring Wendy and check if you like.' She waved nervously at the phone. 'As far as I know, he went straight back to her.' She paused as a thought occurred to her and her brow wrinkled slightly. 'But you know that! You must have seen him come back.'

'We left shortly after you.' For just an instant his grey eyes dropped from hers, but it was enough to give her an inkling of where he had been all night.

'You swine!' Gone was the effort to mollify him and she was now as angry as he was, straining up to him with all her might as her breath came in a low hiss through tight-clenched teeth. 'You accuse me of having Simon here when all the time you've been with Claudia! Talk about double standards!'

'As it happens, I took Claudia and her father straight home and left them on the doorstep.' His eyes were lethal. 'I had a burst tyre on the way back and the spare was missing. I've spent most of the night in the middle of a deserted stretch of road with just my imagination to keep me company.'

'I don't believe you!'

'I don't care what you believe!'

'You really must think I was born yesterday.' Her voice was biting, and a dark red flush forced its way under his high cheekbones and lit his eyes with sinister rage. He looked for all the world like a great black panther seconds before the kill.

'I've a good mind to take you back to my country and teach you what being a woman really means,' he snarled furiously. 'You need to be taught respect.'

'And how would you do that? Beat me, whip me—I can just imagine!' She was beyond fear now.

'Not at all; there are other ways to subdue a rebellious female.' His eyes trailed over her body insolently. 'Especially ones like you.'

'Like me!' She smiled bitterly. 'Well, you might not think much of me, but at least I don't use people for my own gratification and then discard them when I feel like it.'

'Meaning I do?' He gave a small, hard laugh. 'I take it you are referring to the women in my past? No doubt you have been fully informed as to their number and the circumstances of each bitter encounter! Haven't you got the sense to realise that such things are grossly exaggerated and often without a grain of truth?'

'No, but then according to you I haven't got much sense, have I? Though I know one thing.' She paused. His rage seemed to be ebbing and irritation taking its place. 'Most women still want the normal things out of a relationship if they care anything at all about the man: tenderness, being cared for and considered, and eventually marriage and a home and children.'

'Not the women I know.' His voice was curt and cold. 'I made a fool of myself once in that line; never again. You're talking about love and I've been there; it's a road to hell. The women I know want power and influence, and if they are honest about it I can live with that.'

She stood silently looking up at his grim face as the anger left her body in a great flood. She had never been in the presence of such bitter cynicism before; something in his past had seared into his being like a deep wound, and the scar-tissue was so thick that nothing could get through. He had built an impregnable wall around himself, a solid barrier that was unbreakable.

'I think you'd better go,' she whispered quietly.

He nodded slowly as his eyes took in her pallor. 'I should never have come; it was madness. It's just that on that road the pictures that were flashing in my mind...' He turned away sharply as though regretting having said too much. 'You're right, I have no reason to be here.'

'Cord.' She touched his arm hesitantly as he moved away. 'You *are* wrong, you know. Not just about me but life in general. Everyone's not the way you think.'

'Aren't they?' Just for a second there was burning tortured longing written across the hard features, and then he shrugged wearily. 'Well, it doesn't really matter anyway. Nothing lasts; it's all tinsel and glitter.'

'Please, Cord, listen.' She looked up at him with eyes that were suddenly tender, forgetting his rage and the things he had said before. He was hurting inside and she was powerless to help him. 'Give people a chance—open up.'

'You, you mean?' His eyes were cruel again as the wall was cemented firmly in place. He shook his head cynically. 'I like my life the way it is, no commitments and no entanglements.'

'Don't you ever want to have children, marry?'

He laughed in mocking harshness. 'Produce little carbon copies of myself, you mean? That must be the ultimate vanity. Besides which, I've never yet met a woman I would trust to be the mother of my children.'

His gaze tightened broodily and a small twisted smile touched his mouth. 'Why, little dove, are you thinking of applying for the job?'

'No.'

'Maybe you should; I could give you a trial.' His narrowed eyes probed the towelling robe and she pulled it more tightly round her. 'You certainly qualify on some points.'

'Goodnight, Cord.' Her voice was expressionless; he mustn't see how the hunger in those grey eyes was affecting her. It was just a physical release for him; it meant nothing.

He looked at her for a long, silent moment before he reached out and pulled her abruptly into his arms. She began to struggle wildly, vitally aware that she must fight him with her mind before her body proved weak.

'You want me, you know you want me. I can read it in your eyes.' His voice was soft against her hair and she felt dwarfed by his height and male strength and helplessly feminine, as though he was her protector, but then, it wasn't protection he was offering.

'I don't.' His mouth closed over hers as she spoke, parting her lips effortlessly and causing sweet, hot sensation to tingle down her spine as he pulled her closer into him while she continued to twist and turn, knowing that if she didn't resist now she would be lost. He was right, she did want him desperately, but not just for one night or a few weeks until his desire was sated. If she gave herself to him she wanted it to be forever, with enough love on both sides for it to work, and there were times when he didn't even like her! This animal passion of his was something apart.

He was breathing hard as she moved against him in an effort to escape, and then with a hoarse broken cry he lifted her off the ground as she beat with impotent fists against his steel chest. 'I need to get you out of my system,' he said thickly as he carried her towards the bedroom. 'I know what you are but it doesn't seem to make any difference. I can't carry on like this, seeing you every day, wanting you——' As she tried to reply, his mouth tasted hers again, forcing her head backwards against his arm with his passion. She could feel her bones turning to water as desire coursed hot and strong through her throbbing veins, and she arched in his arms frantically, fighting herself rather than him.

He fell with her still wrapped in his arms on to the bed and for a moment she was tempted to succumb to the need that was threatening to consume both of them. 'I won't hurt you, Aline.' He had lifted his face to look at her with blazing hungry eyes as he held her down with the weight of his body. 'It will be good for both of us.' He looked very dark and very powerful against the whiteness of the sheets, and her heart lurched with a mixture of fear and desire as he lowered his head to move down to the hollow of her throat where a pulse was beating frenziedly, and still further as her heartbeat roared in her ears.

There was a gentleness in his passion now that forced a deep, shuddering sigh from her very being and she moaned softly in his imprisoning arms as a shaft of exquisite pleasure shot through her body. She was in the hands of a master craftsman and her innocence was a snare against herself. She didn't know how to resist him and she didn't want to; she loved him, she loved him so much.

'I didn't want it to be like this . . .' She was murmuring to herself as his hands and mouth worked their sensual magic. 'I thought it would be different . . .'

'What?' He became still for a moment against her body as her dazed voice penetrated the fever that had him in its grip. 'What do you mean, you thought it would be different?' A frown twisted the dark face as he lifted himself slightly and stared down at her lying beneath him. 'With me, you mean?'

She looked up at him guilelessly and he read the answer in her innocently bewildered eyes. 'I don't believe it.' His voice was a disbelieving whisper as he froze above her, fighting the knowledge that was dawning in his face. 'You mean you were serious when you said you had never slept with a man before? You can't be. Not at your age, with your looks. Answer me, Aline, and tell me the truth. Were you lying then?'

'I haven't lied to you.' Her voice was very small and he sat up slowly, thrusting her away from him with an almost violent gesture of repudiation.

'I don't believe this is happening.' There was a virtually comical look of shocked amazement written over his dark features as he moved to the side of the bed, rebuttoning his shirt as he spoke. 'And yet I really do believe you for once.' He was speaking as though to himself without looking at her. 'That would tie up with the other night at my house. You were frightened of me?' He asked the question tightly as a small pulse throbbed madly in his throat.

She couldn't reply; there was a huge lump in her chest that was stopping her breathing and as he turned to her, a look of enquiry in his eyes, she shrugged silently. She could hardly tell him that one word of love from him and she would have been his then and forever; it wasn't what he wanted to hear. It hadn't been fear that had driven her out of the house and on to the beach that night, but the knowledge that he was merely using her, that she was just one of a long line, another notch on his belt.

'So Simon *is* just a friend?'

'I told you.' She was bright pink with humiliation and embarrassment as he stared down at her, an enigmatic expression on his face. This had to be the perfect end to a perfect evening! The feeling of rejection had her stomach twisting in knots.

'You've told me a lot of things, but quite honestly, sweetheart, I've taken them all with a pinch of salt.' The old sardonic note was back in the caustic voice but there was something that didn't add up in the watchful grey eyes as she turned over on to her side in a little ball, her hair spread out like a shining veil over her hot, distraught face.

'Well, my little dove, this is a first.' She heard the throb of wry amusement in his voice with a mixture of relief and annoyance. It didn't seem to bother him unduly that his intentions had been thwarted, and she found that this reaction hurt her. She was still shaking from head to foot, and he seemed as cool as a cucumber. 'It might not mean much to you, but there aren't many women who are capable of surprising me these days.'

She risked a quick glance at him and saw there was an unusually tender gleam in the hard grey eyes as he looked down at her, and his hands were not as steady as they might have been as they pulled his tie into position. She suddenly felt immeasurably better.

'I'm beginning to think it was a bad day for me when you exploded into my life, Miss Aline Marcell.' He stood up and walked across the room to the doorway, where he turned to look at her regretfully.

'I'm sorry.' It was weak but all she could manage. In spite of the rough stubbly shadow on his square chin, the rumpled clothes and untidy hair, he had never looked more desirable to her. There was something in his eyes she couldn't fathom, but she liked it.

'I think I'd better leave while I still can.' She stared back at him in breathless silence. Something had happened between them in the last few minutes and she could almost feel him fighting it. 'You're OK?' She nodded in reply and he repeated the gesture slowly. 'Good. I'll see you on Monday as usual.' She thought there was a slight emphasis on the last two words, and then he left.

She heard his firm, measured footsteps cross the other room, the front door open and close, and then she was alone. She lay just as he had left her while her heartbeat slowed to normal and the hot flush that had stained her fair skin melted away.

Why hadn't he taken her? The thought was jabbing at her mind. He had had the power to do so and he knew it, so why had he stopped in time? Maybe inexperienced women didn't do anything for him? She moved restlessly; no, that wasn't it. The raging hunger had been there in his eyes just the same as he had stared at her across the room seconds before he left. He wanted her all right.

It was more likely that he didn't think she was worth complicating their working relationship for. It was one thing to have a casual affair with a woman who was used to such things, but quite another to have an innocent on his conscience. She thought about his last few words: 'as usual'. The words took on a distinct importance. He had been trying to tell her all this meant nothing to him, that was it! She rolled over on the bed and pulled the pillow across her face in an effort to still her bewildered thoughts and stop the post-mortem on the last half-hour.

Whatever his reason, it didn't make any difference to the unpleasant truth she must face day after day. She loved a man who thought she was a thief and by his own admission didn't believe a word she said. It was all suddenly too much. Every accusation he had ever made returned in perfect clarity to haunt her, and the fact that she had caught a glimpse of a different side to him tonight for a few seconds, a tenderness she had never expected, made it all so much harder to bear. The sooner the required year of servitude was over, the better, but what state would she be reduced to when she was finally free to leave him for good?

CHAPTER SEVEN

THE next few weeks were the worst of Aline's life. She had been dreading going into work on the following Monday morning after Cord's visit to her apartment, but her worst fears couldn't have imagined the sight that met her eyes as she walked into his office early that morning before the others had arrived. She had been hoping for a quick private word with Cord to clear the air between them, and after seeing his car parked outside she had hurried into the general office and through to her room without looking to left or right, opening his door quietly in case he was on the phone.

He wasn't, though. He was sitting in his chair behind his desk with Claudia wrapped so tightly round him as she sat on his lap that it was a wonder that either of them could breathe, especially in view of the way she was kissing him so passionately. Aline stood there for one stunned moment, unable to drag her eyes away from the sight that was tearing her heart out by the roots, and in the same instant his eyes met hers over the top of Claudia's head and widened in startled disbelief. She was aware that he stood up as she turned away into her own room, and it was evident from the thud of a falling body that his arms hadn't been holding the redhead to him, but as she fled across the few yards into the general office she didn't stop to answer his hoarse cry.

Some time later when the others arrived she had gained enough composure to leave the ladies' powder-room and take her place at her desk as though nothing had happened. He had tried to speak to her about it that morning

127

but she had cut him dead with one sharply scathing glance. 'What you do or don't do is nothing to do with me,' she had said coldly as soul-destroying jealousy had gripped her with tight, burning fingers. 'You don't have to apologise to me for your actions.'

'I wasn't going to apologise for *my* actions,' he had answered in a deep, harsh voice, but she had jerked her head aside as he went to continue and walked out into her own office. He hadn't followed her but she had heard him swear fluently as he had slammed the door shut after her. It was foolish to feel so hurt and betrayed; he hadn't promised her anything, had he? He was a free agent at liberty to kiss whoever he wanted. If only it had been anyone but Claudia! But no, that wasn't quite true. This agonising, paralysing misery would have been as painful whoever she had seen him with.

The days dragged by into weeks and one Monday morning Aline was surprised to realise it was late November, with the fierce heat of the summer months a distant memory. Cord had maintained a distant, businesslike attitude over the last few weeks, allowing her to leave on time with the others each night and displaying no interest in her private life at all. She, on the other hand, regularly lay awake half the night while her imagination painted wild pictures of him and Claudia locked in one passionate embrace after another, and in consequence her slenderness became more pronounced, producing an ethereality that added to rather than subtracted from her pale silver beauty.

'I'm having a barbecue at the weekend for my staff and a few friends.' She had just shrugged her jacket off and was tidying her hair into the neat chignon she had tried for the first time that morning, before starting work on the mountain of papers on her desk that greeted her after every weekend. She couldn't believe one man could generate so much work; he must hardly ever sleep.

She turned quickly as the deep voice spoke from the doorway of Cord's office, her hands still to her hair in that age-old feminine gesture that Renaissance painters loved to capture, her brown eyes wide and startled. As his dark grey eyes flicked lightly over her face she noticed with surprise that he was looking tired and drawn; it had been some time since she had actually stared into his face. It was less painful that way.

'Come in a moment, would you, Aline?' His voice was bland and the austere cold face imperturbable as she followed him quietly into the room, standing silently before him while he seated himself at the big desk awash with correspondence.

'I've noticed that the English contingent keep very much to themselves; there is no problem that you are aware of?'

She shook her head slowly as she forced her mind to detach itself from the sight of the big lithe body leaning back in the large leather seat. Any other man would be dwarfed by the huge chair but it fitted his long hard frame quite comfortably. 'I don't think so; we just don't seem to have integrated very well, I'm afraid, although the French staff are very friendly.'

'Nevertheless I am anxious that everyone should get to know each other better; it was probably a mistake to house all the English employees together but what is done is done. I've been meaning to organise a get-together to break the ice for some time, but other priorities have got in the way.' A mental image of Claudia's sleek body flashed into her mind and a chill sensation feathered over her flesh.

'Anyway, I have decided to buy the house on the coast, so I feel free to open it up for the weekend. There's plenty of room for everyone to stay overnight, although obviously some of the French employees would prefer to return home anyway.' She nodded to show she was listening as her insides shrunk. No doubt Claudia would be searingly present, and two days of watching them together was not tempting.

'I shall expect everyone to attend, at least for the Saturday night barbecue. Let them know, would you?' He lowered his black head dismissively and she felt a tiny spurt of rebellion leap in her. He really did act like one of the old archaic monarchs at times, manipulating his subjects with no consideration for their opinions or desires. It might have something to do with his fierce and turbulent Corsican heritage, but today it grated on her like barbed wire on silk.

No one else shared her misgivings. Everyone was thrilled at the thought of a free weekend in luxurious surroundings and she could tell that more than one female was secretly curious to see where Cord lived. He was an enigma to his employees, a fascinatingly sensual man who never showed the slightest interest in even the most attractive of his female staff, and any insight into that cool, powerful mind was irresistible to most of them.

On the Thursday before the barbecue she was surprised by a knock on her front door as she was getting ready to leave for the office. She opened it quickly, her eyes widening in amazement.

'Cord?' It was the first time she had voluntarily spoken his name in weeks, and she couldn't hide the hot flush flooding her pale cheeks.

'Good morning, Aline.' His voice was cool and dispassionate as he shot her a swift all-encompassing glance. 'We have a minor problem.'

'We do?' Stop it, Aline, she berated herself sharply, you sound like a complete idiot. She schooled her features into a polite smile and took a deep steadying breath. 'Come in, won't you? I was just finishing a cup of coffee. Would you like one?'

'I'd love one.' He followed her into the room and stood leaning against the small breakfast-bar, watching her as she poured him some coffee and refilled her own cup. She felt she needed its boost—blow the caffeine!

'What's the problem?' His warm hand touched hers when he took the cup from her and she felt an electric shock run up her arm and set her nerves quivering as he settled himself in an easy chair before replying.

'Difficulties with one of the suppliers. I'm not sure if it's a genuine predicament or if one particular man is trying to cause trouble. There is no way I can delegate on this one; I need to go and see the situation for myself and fast. It would be helpful if you accompanied me; there will be certain points you can help with, which I'll explain on the way. OK?'

'You mean now?' she asked haltingly.

He looked at her quietly but she noticed that those grey eyes darkened fractionally. 'Of course.'

'Yes, that's fine; I'll phone in and explain and——'

He cut into her stammerings smoothly. 'That's all taken care of; just finish your coffee and we'll be off. I have all the relevant correspondence in the car and it will take us some time to reach our destination.'

Once on the road Cord drove swiftly and with intense concentration, leaving her free to pursue her own thoughts. The serene landscape through which they were travelling was decked in autumn splendour, although it was far from cold, and as they went deeper into the French countryside she could feel history oozing from the cool cream stone of elegant houses, from the crumbling ancient walls still surrounding many towns and villages and from the old weathered farm buildings clearly visible on what was becoming a smooth, flat landscape. They passed numerous châteaux that mirrored the history of the land, from the grim, austere fortresses of the Middle Ages to the magical, flamboyant palaces of the seventeenth and eighteenth centuries. Aline was sorry when they eventually drew into the small town where Cord's business was to be conducted, and her face must have shown her disappointment because he touched her hand lightly as he helped her out of the car, and she saw he was smiling down at her.

'Business first, pleasure later,' he whispered enigmatically as a delegation of smiling Frenchmen hurried from the glass-panelled reception area of the small office building.

As it happened, their visit was a short one. It transpired that the main problem was a breakdown in communication, which, once righted, brought the other difficulties under control fairly easily. Cord refused their offer of lunch with a polite smile and within an hour they were back in the car and on the road again.

'Hungry?' He spoke with his eyes on the twisting road ahead and Aline looked at the dark hard profile hesitantly.

'A little.'

'Well, I'm starving. There's a place I've had it in mind to show you for some time; I think you'll like it.'

She found she was staring at him and hastily glanced away. Had it in mind to show her for some time. What did that mean? He had given no indication over the last little while that he was even aware of her existence most of the time. She sat in bemused silence. He really was the most puzzling man.

'The great writer, François Rabelais, was born round here,' Cord said after a while. 'Have you read his works?'

'No.' She shook her head. 'Have you?'

'No.' He smiled warmly. 'We're two ignoramuses together, then. It's just that I understand that the more prosaic appetites he symbolises are perfect for this region; the pleasure the locals gain from good wine and food is legendary. I've only visited this part of France a few times but I always leave with a full stomach and a happy memory.'

She nodded smilingly to hide the sudden lurch her own stomach made. No doubt he had been with Claudia those other times.

'Here we are.' They had driven into a small well-kept courtyard festooned with flowers with a large stone building on three sides. 'This is the best restaurant in the area, and that's saying something.'

He led her through a wide-open door and for a moment she blinked as the bright sunlight outside was replaced by shadowed warmth. They were in what appeared to be an old hall, with a blazing log fire at one end and a few scattered tables and chairs placed in pleasing harmony round a central bar. The old stained-glass windows and beamed ceiling overhead added to the general impression of a medieval banqueting hall, as did the hanging tapestries and ancient weapons adorning the stone walls.

'Unusual, isn't it?' He seemed pleased with her wide-eyed reaction. 'But wait till you taste the food.'

When the meal came she realised he hadn't exaggerated. He had insisted she try the *brochet au beurre blanc*, which turned out to be pike served with a wonderfully creamy sauce made from butter, warmed and flavoured with wine, vinegar and shallots. It was delectable, especially when eaten with stuffed mushrooms served on a small side-plate and washed down with Muscadet, a dry white wine of the region.

'Good, eh?' Cord was watching her rapt enjoyment of the food with quiet delight, and she nodded her agreement.

'These mushrooms are absolutely gorgeous.'

'They're grown in large underground galleries that used to be old quarry-workings round here. I understand the caves supply half of France.' They continued to make small talk while they ate and for the first time since she had known him Aline found herself beginning to relax in his company, although remaining vitally aware of every small move that lazy, controlled body made.

It was as they were drinking coffee that he brought Claudia's name into the conversation, although the tall redhead's spectre had been at Aline's elbow all through the delicious meal. 'I want to clear the air before the barbecue, Aline.' She glanced up in surprise and caught a faintly anxious look in the narrowed grey eyes before a shutter came down.

'Yes?' Her nerves tightened.

'That morning in the office with Claudia—I wasn't kissing her; it wasn't how it seemed.'

'Cord, you don't have to explain——'

'Just shut up, Aline.' The bark was back in his voice and she subsided into silence as he took a long, deep breath. 'You aren't making this any easier.'

'I'm so sorry.' She couldn't stop the thread of sarcasm from showing and he cast her an exasperated frown before continuing.

'I repeat, I wasn't kissing her. The little incident you interrupted was just Claudia's way of saying thank you for a favour I had done her father.'

'It must have been a big favour.' She didn't even try to hide the sarcasm this time and he frowned at her in irritated annoyance.

'She's French; they do things differently over here.'

She was about to reply with a very rude comment but contented herself with an explosive 'Huh!' instead.

'Don't you believe me?' There was steel in the dark face now but she had been hurt once too often to care.

'No.'

'I see; well, in that case there is nothing more to be said, is there? Would you care for more coffee?'

'No, thank you.' The easy relaxed mood had been shattered into a million pieces and she felt like bursting into tears. Why hadn't she met him halfway? Blow Claudia! Even when she wasn't around she was still causing trouble.

The sky was turning grey on the drive home and it looked as though it might rain. The weather matched her mood; a bleak hopelessness had settled on her, turning the beautiful countryside dull and locking her deep inside herself. Cord was totally silent by her side, but without the comfortable relaxation he had displayed on the drive down.

They arrived back at the office mid-afternoon and she worked frantically for the rest of the day, grateful to have something definite to channel her mind into. It was with a dark feeling of inevitability that she heard the unmistakable click of Claudia's heels in the outer office just before she was due to go home.

'You're back, then.' Claudia's eyes were narrowed into pale slits in her beautiful face and her gaze was openly hostile as Aline glanced up. She clearly knew about, and resented, their trip.

'As you can see.' For once Aline didn't try to disguise her dislike of the lovely redhead, and her voice was tart as their eyes locked across the room.

'What time did you get back?'

Aline shrugged casually as she lowered her glance to the papers on her desk. 'I don't remember; ask Mr

Lachoni.' There was a moment of silence as loud as thunder and then Claudia swept past her into Cord's office in a wave of expensive perfume and outraged pride, her face venomous. She was still closeted in there half an hour later when Aline left once the others had gone; she hadn't wanted company tonight.

As she wandered through the quiet streets in the light, refreshing rain she felt her hot tears mingle with the water on her face. 'Cord . . . How could you?' She stopped for a minute and looked up into the grey sky as a million tiny raindrops fell plummeting to earth. 'With her of all people.' But then cold reason stepped in. Claudia was rich, she was beautiful and she adored him; how could any man resist her? It was all hopeless.

The day of the barbecue dawned bright and sunny, much to Aline's disgust. She had been hoping, childishly, that the rain would continue, but it had cleared magically overnight and the air was several degrees warmer in consequence. 'Even the weather does what he wants,' she muttered wearily to herself as she got ready later that afternoon.

It was just five o'clock when Aline emerged with some of the English crowd from one of the taxis Cord had ordered for them all, and already lights were twinkling in the still warm air in the long, sloping garden that led down to the beach. She found herself stiff with tension, her slender body rigid in the cornflower-blue silk dress and jacket she had bought especially for the evening, and her dark eyes widened with apprehension.

'Let's get a drink.' Simon slipped an arm round her waist and pulled Wendy close to him with his other arm as the three of them walked over to the long bar at one side of the wide patio.

The tall, dark figure standing in the shadows watched them walk from the car and join the crowd on the patio and his face didn't relax until Simon's hand left her waist, and then the look in the hard grey eyes wasn't pleasant.

'Hello, Aline.' She turned to greet him with a polite smile but it froze on her face as her eyes registered the coldness in Cord's tight gaze.

'Is anything wrong?' He smiled slowly and there was something almost predatory in his eyes.

'Not exactly.' As the others moved further down the garden he took her arm in a firm grip, moving her slowly into the house. 'I want a word with you, that's all.' The big french windows were open and as he led her through the sitting-room she noticed Claudia standing in a laughing animated group, her opaque eyes narrowing as Cord briefly acknowledged her wave before opening another door and leading Aline through, shutting it after him with a loud click.

She found herself in his study and noticed with a wry inward smile that his desk here was as untidy as the one in the office. 'Yes?' She looked up into his dark face as she spoke but he seated himself quietly on the desk, crossing his arms and considering her with eyes that could have been forged in steel.

'Don't you think it's unfair to lead Simon on the way you do?' His tone was almost conversational, and it took a moment for the content of his words to register in her brain.

'I beg your pardon!'

'I don't think I need to repeat myself,' he said smoothly, his voice soft and low. 'I just don't want the spectacle of you leading him round with a ring in his nose to ruin the weekend for everyone. It's... undignified.'

'There are times, Cord, when I think you live on a different planet from the rest of us!'

Surprise glowed momentarily in the hard eyes. He had clearly expected her reaction to be different. 'Am I supposed to know what that means?' he asked slowly.

'You must be the only person in the office who doesn't know that he's crazy about Wendy,' she said coldly as two bright spots of colour began to burn in her cheeks. 'It's been obvious for months.'

His glance narrowed suddenly and he slid off the desk abruptly, moving to her side. 'Are you telling me the truth?'

'Oh, for goodness' sake!' She could feel her patience beginning to ebb. 'What's it to do with you anyway? If you don't believe me, just ask anyone! They are an item, a couple—call it anything you want.'

'I see.' There was a touch of dark red colour under his cheekbones and for once he seemed nonplussed, his eyes falling away from her furious gaze as he turned towards the closed door. 'Well, there's no problem, then. I just didn't want him getting hurt.'

'You cheeky——' Words failed her as she glared at his straight back. 'Even if he was interested in me, who's to say he would get hurt? And why the sudden concern about Simon anyway? You're not his father.'

'No, you're quite right, I'm not his father.' She took a step backwards as he turned round with his hand on the doorknob. There was something dangerous in his eyes. 'That sharp little tongue of yours is going to get you into trouble one day.'

The sheer injustice of it all turned her eyes hard and forced her chin up to meet his gaze. 'Have you quite finished?' Her voice was icy and proud and she saw the tone register on his face. 'I'd like to get back to the real people now.'

'Would you?' he parried softly. 'I think you are in danger of forgetting something very important, my cool

little dove. I have bought you for a year and you are
only enjoying freedom at this moment because I stayed
my hand regarding your devious... activities. You for-
feited all your rights when you helped yourself to my
money and I am perfectly at liberty to demand that you
account for every minute of every day if I so choose.
Clear?'

'Yes.' The last tiny vestige of sweetness that had hung
in her memory from the night at her apartment disappeared, melting in the heat of his burning gaze. She had
imagined the tenderness; it couldn't have been real. This
was real, this bitterly cruel man with his piercingly cold
eyes and sharp tongue that could reduce her to nothing
in seconds.

'Good. I see we understand each other.' He beckoned
her insultingly with a jerk of his head and she moved to
stand in front of him, her cheeks burning. 'Just to make
sure...' As he lowered his head and took her lips in a
cool gesture of mastery she forced herself to remain still
and unresponsive under his touch, her hands clenched
into small tight fists by her side. There was no gentleness
in the kiss; it was intended as a lesson in obedience, a
message that he held the whip hand. She didn't know
when the tempo of the hard mouth on hers changed,
but suddenly his arms pulled her into his body and he
groaned softly as his lips became coaxingly sensual.

For a moment everything in her leapt to respond to
the hard desire she could feel in the male body so close
to hers, but then his cold uncaring words echoed jar-
ringly in her brain like a dash of cold water in her face,
and she kept herself rigidly still, her mouth still under
his caressing lips and her arms limp by her sides. She
could feel his heart thudding furiously as he whispered
her name, and as she still didn't respond his breathing
grew harsh. Another second and she would have to reach

up and pull his hard frame closer to her; this torment was driving her mad.

'Get out!' He had let go of her so suddenly that she almost whimpered with disappointment, but then as his words hit home and she looked into his dark face she opened the door swiftly, hearing it bang behind her as she fled across the room outside, blind to the curious glances that followed her.

She found she was shaking uncontrollably as the cool night air washed over her hot face. She heard one or two people call her name but merely raised a hand in casual salute, intent on finding somewhere, anywhere to hide.

'Where are you rushing off to?' Wendy caught hold of her arm laughingly as she passed the crowd clustered round the smoking barbecue where juicy man-sized steaks sizzled gently in their nest of onions and mushrooms. Her expression changed as she noticed the naked pain in Aline's dark eyes. 'What's happened?' Wendy led her away quickly to a quiet secluded corner, pushing her down gently on to a long wooden bench and sitting close by her side. 'It's Mr Lachoni, isn't it—you've fallen for him?'

Aline looked at her bleakly. 'Is it that obvious?'

'It's not obvious at all, I promise.' Wendy's face held a mixture of concern and dismay. 'But it *is* crazy, Aline! He isn't the sort of guy you fall in love with, not unless you've got a death wish.'

'I know, I know, don't tell me.' Aline waved her hand weakly as she took some long deep breaths to clear her head. 'I'm being ridiculous; don't worry about it. Come on.' She stood up and pulled at Wendy's arm, leading her back towards the lights. The last thing she felt capable of tonight was discussing her emotions with anyone. 'I'm famished—let's eat.'

Nothing could have been further from the truth, but she did feel more in control after forcing down a few mouthfuls of steak and drinking a glass of light sparkling wine.

Cord had spared no expense to ensure everyone had a good time. The caterers were more than generous in their determination to load everyone's plates again and again and keep the wine glasses brimming. A small band arrived just after everyone had eaten, quickly setting up their instruments on the small stage Cord had provided. Soon the night air was full of music as more and more couples began to dance.

She had caught the odd glimpse of Cord's tall, powerful figure as he circulated smilingly among his guests, Claudia hanging like a human limpet on his arm, but each time she had dropped her eyes immediately in case their glances should meet. She began to get the impression that he was avoiding her, certainly he didn't stray into her orbit, and as the night progressed she began to relax a little, forcing herself to dance with the succession of young men who vied fiercely for her favours.

'Are you enjoying yourself?' There was no mistaking that heavily accented voice and she turned to meet Claudia's cold gaze head-on. 'May I join you?' The frosty eyes were expressionless.

'Of course.' Aline waved a hand for Claudia to be seated at the small table out of the main throng where she had been catching her breath and enjoying a long chilled glass of lemonade as she watched the others dancing. 'I'm just resting for a moment.'

'Yes, I noticed you have been much in demand.' Claudia managed to make the ordinary words full of subtle insult. 'Quite the belle of the ball, as Cord remarked.' The pale blue eyes were vicelike.

'Did he?' Aline said carefully. She sensed there was more to come.

'I told him that young girls should enjoy themselves while they can; it's not long before they get to be boring old couples like us.' The redhead laughed lightly as she flicked back a lock of russet hair from her smooth white shoulders. She was dressed in a sleeveless black silk catsuit that showed her magnificent figure off to full advantage, the low neck only just within the bounds of propriety and the dark material clinging to her flesh like a second skin.

'We're only young once.' Aline kept her voice sweet as she delivered the slight to the other woman's maturity and steeled herself mentally for the onslaught. This wasn't just a friendly little chat; there was something glowing in those pale reptilian eyes that was positively fiendish. The snub registered on the beautiful face and Claudia stiffened slowly.

'Has he told you he's buying the house?'

'Yes, he mentioned it.' Aline forced herself to smile coolly. 'It's a lovely place.'

'*I* like it.' The soft purr was back, dripping honey. 'I wanted somewhere that was still close to Daddy after we—— Oops! Nearly let the cat out of the bag, as you English say.' She twisted her curvaceous body gently in the seat, pouting prettily. 'That's me, I'm afraid, can't keep a secret to save my life.'

'Oh, I'm sure you could if you tried.' It was weak but all Aline could manage through her closed throat. Her heart was hammering against her ribs and her mouth was desperately dry.

The diamond-hard eyes watched her silently, considering the effect of her words. 'I haven't shocked you, have I? You surely knew that Cord and I are...more than friends?'

Aline looked at the French woman without trying to hide the distaste in her face. 'That's none of my business, surely?'

'You're so right.' Claudia rose slowly, stretching gracefully like a beautiful, lazy cat. 'I shall enjoy living here.' She glanced down at Aline as she spoke, her hair a flame of red in the lights and her eyes glittering like ice in her lovely face. 'It will be a good place to bring up children, don't you think?' She smiled in satisfaction at Aline's sudden sharp intake of breath and smoothed the silk over her hips contentedly.

'It's a lovely place,' Aline repeated dully as she struggled to keep her face bland.

'I'd better go and see if he needs me.' Claudia sauntered off unhurriedly as she spoke, adding over her shoulder for good measure, 'He never likes me to leave him for too long.'

Aline stared after the tall redhead as her lacerated nerves sprang into painful life. So that was what it was all about: he was going to marry her. She should have guessed. The forging of the new business alliance with Claudia's father, the acquisition of a sumptuous house in France that was far too big for one man to live in alone, the evenings spent at the Asvana home... She had been such a fool! All the signs had been there, but she had been too stupid to read them.

She found her hands were clenched together so tightly that her fingernails were grooving weals into her flesh, and with a supreme effort of will she forced herself to relax, drawing the breath into her chest in long, deep gasps as though she had been running a race.

She had known tonight was going to be a disaster; she should have feigned illness and stayed at home. She raised her head and glanced wildly round the brilliantly lit garden, amazed to see that everything looked just the same as before Claudia had dropped her bombshell. More couples were wandering inside now as the chill of the night began to make itself felt, but she didn't seem able to feel anything except the pain that was threatening to take over her senses. She must get away for a while. The beach—yes, she could walk there unhindered and out of sight. No one would miss her for an hour or so.

She slipped away quietly, her blue dress blending into the velvet blackness as she reached the beach. Tiny grains of white sand crept into her sandals and she bent down to take them off, swinging them in her hands as she resumed walking, the sand cold and soft under her bare feet.

If only she could walk back to England along this beach. Walk back to the safe, ordinary existence she had known before this dark meteor had shot into her life, like a brilliant black shooting star that destroyed everything in its path and left a broken trail of devastation in its wake. If only... But then life was full of 'if only's, and she must concentrate on the hard facts.

The man she loved disliked and despised her and was going to marry someone else. There was nothing for her now, and this barren, empty feeling deep inside would grow and grow with the years until no one would remember that once she had been young and beautiful and in love with life.

CHAPTER EIGHT

'YOU'RE going to freeze again.' Cord's firm mouth was curved in a strange smile as Aline swung round to face him in the darkness, and his teeth shone white in the bronze of his face. 'This is getting to be a habit.' He stood looking down at her silently, the sounds of the party muted and blurred in the distance and the sea a soft swish by their feet. 'What are you doing out here?' He took a step closer to look tightly into her face. 'You've been crying.'

'I felt like a walk, that's all.' She glanced behind him quickly. 'Where's Claudia?'

'How should I know?' he replied irritably, his eyes intent on her white face. 'I'm not her keeper.'

She shrugged her shoulders as she tore her gaze away from his. 'Well, she hasn't left your side all night, I just thought——'

'You just thought what?' His teeth gleamed again but this time the smile held light mockery. 'Not jealous, are you?'

'Jealous!' She was glad the darkness hid her rising colour as she turned away. 'Hardly.'

'You're quite right, it was a ridiculous suggestion.' There was acid in the deep voice and she was aware that she had touched a sore spot. Good. She would like to hurt him after the pain he had inflicted on her tonight.

'No doubt you prefer the company of those young clowns you were dancing with back there?'

She met his eyes and saw that his dark face was set in harsh lines, making his thoughts impossible to read.

'Yes, as it happens.' She had thrown caution to the wind; there was nothing to lose now. 'They were good fun, they were friendly and they liked me. What's wrong with that?'

His expression revealed that she had not given him the answer he had expected, and after a moment's silence his mouth twisted into an ugly sneer. 'Honesty? At this late stage? Well, well.' He folded his arms as he stared down at her with narrowed cold eyes. 'And would you have danced with me if I had requested such an honour?'

'There was no danger of that, was there?' she answered quietly as she turned to look up into the charcoal-smudged sky, praying he wouldn't hear the thudding of her heart. 'I might get ideas above my station if you granted me such a rare privilege, and besides, Claudia wouldn't like it.'

'Claudia again.' His voice was thoughtful and he suddenly reached out and turned her round so that she was held in front of him, imprisoned by his vicelike grip. 'That's twice in as many minutes that you've mentioned that particular lady. Any special reason?'

'You should know.' It sounded childish, but she felt like a small, hurt child. There was something in her that longed to throw herself on the sand in front of him and howl and kick and scream herself hoarse. Why did he play these cruel games? What perverse delight did he get in seeing her squirm?

'Let's pretend for a minute that I don't.' There was that scratching tight note in his voice that indicated his patience was running out; she had heard it too often since working with him not to recognise its bite. She was amazed to find that for once she didn't care if she roused his anger. It was as though the very worst thing that could happen had happened and it had somehow cut something free. 'Let's pretend I'm not very bright and you are going to set me right.'

'Oh, what's the point?' She tried to fling herself aside but his grip was too hard, and instead she was jerked against him for a brief moment, her breasts soft against the hardness of his body. She felt him tense and he carefully moved her to arm's length again, and his face was tight when he next spoke.

'The point is, I want to know! Now, I understand you probably can't wait to get back to all your admirers, but please restrain yourself for just a few minutes and answer me in language I can understand, and then I'll remove my unwelcome presence from you as quickly as I can.'

'My admirers!' She glared up at him. 'At least they *are* just friends and I don't skulk around after dark having my fun. If I cared about someone enough to marry them, I wouldn't be ashamed to say so, and I certainly wouldn't lie about it.'

'I gather that's a dig against me, but you are going to have to be more specific.' His voice was steel-hard now and his fingers bit into the soft flesh of her upper arms.

'You're hurting me.' She tried to shake herself free again and her hair fell across her face in a shining silver cloud.

'I'd like to!' His face was suddenly savage. 'Believe me, I would really like to, my beautiful little tease. You've done nothing but provoke me all night.'

'I have not!' She bent back slightly in his grasp to look up into the furious face above her. 'You can't possibly accuse me of that; I only saw you once at the beginning when you dragged me into your study.'

'Don't give me that innocent look, it won't wash! You've known exactly what you were doing to me, dancing with those other men, letting them hold you . . .'

His voice was thick and hoarse with dark emotion and
a low groan was wrenched from him as he looked down
at her pale, translucent skin in the moonlight, her half-
open mouth and wide, dark eyes. He swore softly as he
pulled her inexorably closer towards him until she was
crushed tightly against his broad chest.

'Don't.' The casual blue denim shirt he wore was
undone to just above his waist and she could feel rough
black body hair against the smoothness of her skin as
he nuzzled into her hair with his chin. Her legs were
shaking so much that it was only his hands on her body
that were keeping her upright.

'Don't?' He echoed her voice with a sigh. 'The need
to do this has been driving me crazy all night, and you
say, Don't.' He ran his hands possessively over her as
his mouth fired on to hers, and as she felt the hunger
in him her own desire leapt to meet it, taking her un-
awares. He sank down with her on to the sand and the
shudder that swept through his hard frame was felt in
her body as he covered her face in kisses, cradling her
against him as his hands slipped under the thin silk of
her dress to the warm, throbbing flesh beneath. She
jolted with the shock of it, horrified that her body could
let her down so completely in view of all that had gone
before.

'Leave me alone!' This time she took him by surprise
when she jerked away, knocking him on to his back as
she sat up, putting air between them.

His breathing was harsh and laboured as he sat up in
his turn, running a hand over his face while he spoke.
'What the hell is the matter now? I wasn't going to rape
you, for crying out loud!'

'If you want to make love to someone, go and find
Claudia!' She could hear that she was shouting, but she
couldn't stop. 'She *is* the one you're going to marry!

She's the one who is going to live with you in your house!' She was almost incoherent with a mixture of rage and grief, and he looked at her in total amazement as she jumped up wildly, her face drained of colour and her eyes wide and staring.

He was quite still for a moment and then stood up slowly, letting his breath out in a big sigh as he thrust his hands deep into the pockets of his jeans. 'And where did you hear that little piece of juicy gossip?'

'It is not gossip.' She spaced the words out slowly as she lowered her voice. 'Claudia told me herself, this evening. You are buying the house so she can still be near her father after you're married. *She* told me! At least it will save you having to drive her home each night—or perhaps you don't bother? Perhaps Daddy doesn't mind his little girl playing the whore?'

The sound of her own words checked her rage, and she was suddenly mortified by their ugliness. She turned from him, putting her trembling hands to her hot cheeks and shaking her head gently. 'I'm sorry. I shouldn't have said that.' The silence between them lengthened and she didn't dare turn round. 'It's nothing to do with me how you conduct your life and, whatever else she might be, I know Claudia isn't a whore.'

He still didn't speak and at last she looked towards him. He was standing gazing out to sea as though carved in stone, a big frozen statue on the white sand, his bulk black against the midnight-blue sky.

'Cord?' She whispered his name hesitantly; there was something about his stillness that terrified her.

'What do you know about whores?' His voice wasn't angry or loud, just totally devoid of feeling with a dead dullness that frightened her more than all his anger. 'I was married to one for three years, so you could say I'm something of an expert.'

'What?' She wasn't aware she had whispered the word out loud, but she must have done, because he suddenly turned towards her and his face was terrible to behold.

'Oh, she didn't take money for it, understand, nothing so crude as that. No, Megan was paid for her favours with excitement, forbidden thrills, and all under the cover of a wedding-ring. She could make you believe you were the only man on earth in bed, the first and the last, and I thought it was just for me.' He laughed softly but it was like no sound she had ever heard before.

'Even when I found out what she had been doing I still couldn't believe it, but by the time I caught her in bed with my best friend I was beyond caring what she did. I think I even wished him good luck that night; he sure as hell was going to need it.'

She stared at him in horrified silence and he shook his head slightly. 'Go back to the party, Aline.'

'Please, Cord——' She took a step towards him but his eyes were looking at something she couldn't see and he brushed her aside wearily.

'Go back, Aline; go back before I say something I'll regret. We've both said too much as it is.'

She left him standing by the water's edge as she walked slowly along the beach, her head whirling as she tried to take in what she had just been told. This, then, was the cause of his harsh cynicism where the female sex was concerned. She had never stood a chance from the first moment. Why couldn't she have met him before Megan put her poison into his bloodstream? As the lights and noise grew nearer she turned round just once before leaving the beach. He was standing just as she had left him, looking out to sea, a remote black figure on the dark coastline, more distant and unapproachable now than he had ever been.

*   *   *

She didn't want to wake the next day. She heard Wendy rise and use the bathroom in the room they were sharing, and after a few moments the rhythmic drone of the shower lulled her back to sleep. It was so comforting not to have to think or feel.

Some time later she was vaguely aware of someone pulling back the curtains and opening the window so that bright, fresh, salty air streamed into the bedroom, and as a shaft of brilliant sunlight strayed across her face she decided she would have to face the world after all. She opened her eyes slowly, expecting to see Wendy's cheerful face.

Cord was standing to one side of the bed, staring down at her, his big body dark against the white sunlight flooding round him, his face taut and his eyes shadowed. 'Hi.'

Aline gazed up at him in amazement, her mouth a small 'o' of surprise, and after a moment a wry smile twisted the corner of his mouth. 'I'm not going to eat you, although I won't say the idea hasn't occurred to me. It's after twelve; aren't you ever going to get up?'

'It can't be.' She looked round her in bewilderment as she half rose in the bed. 'Where's Wendy?'

'Gone for a walk along the beach with the others, admittedly somewhat reluctantly. I think she'd got the idea I was going to race up here and have my wicked way with you once the coast was clear.' There was dry mockery in the deep voice and she gathered he wasn't altogether pleased.

'Oh.' Her voice was small. 'You should have woken me before.'

'You looked as though you needed the sleep.' His voice was flat. 'I've been working you too hard.'

'Of course you haven't,' she protested quickly, but stiffened as he leant down and touched the faint mauve shadows under her eyes with a gentle finger.

'Well, something is putting those there.'

The gentleness was too much to take and she slid down into the bed again, pulling the covers up to her chin. 'I'll get dressed, then.'

'There's a cold snack in the kitchen when you're ready.' He walked slowly to the door. 'I'll brew some coffee.'

'Thank you.' There was no warmth in the grim face, and she didn't know how she was supposed to react.

He was sitting reading the papers when she entered the kitchen some time later. He threw them to one side, his eyes moving approvingly over the fluffy white jumper and black trousers she was wearing, and fastening on her hair, swinging in a high, shiny pony-tail. 'You look about sixteen with your hair like that,' he said softly. 'Until one takes in the rest of you, of course.'

She blushed furiously and he smiled as he indicated the cold buffet set out to one side of the kitchen. 'No one could face much after last night; help yourself.' She filled a plate with cold meats and salad and he frowned as she sat down by his side. 'You don't eat enough.' She looked up in surprise and caught an oddly tender gleam in the grey eyes before he turned away to pour the coffee.

'Did everyone go for a walk?' She couldn't bring herself to mention Claudia by name, but the vision of the tall, elegant redhead hiking along the beach with Cord's employees just didn't fit. She knew Claudia had intended to stay; she had made a great show of insisting she have the room next to Cord's when he had showed them all around the previous night.

He gazed at her for a moment in enigmatic silence and then spoke lightly, his voice even and dry. 'Claudia had to leave unexpectedly last night; otherwise the party is the same and everyone is out.'

She flushed scarlet and took a hasty sip of the scalding hot coffee, burning the back of her throat in her haste. He knew she had wondered where Claudia was; she felt that quivering in her stomach which his nearness always produced. The man could even read her mind! She forced a polite smile to her lips. 'I hope she isn't unwell?'

He leant back in his chair with a small smile, clearly amused by her duplicity. 'Not as far as I know.'

'Good.'

He rose and filled his own plate, sitting back at the table and eating with every appearance of enjoying the food. Aline felt as though every mouthful was going to choke her. She should be immune from the effect of those clear grey eyes but one glance had the power to turn her into spineless jelly. He, on the other hand, clearly had no such handicap where she was concerned.

She was enormously thankful when the others returned a few minutes later and they all drifted, as a group, into the garden. The rest of the day flew by and she took great care to avoid Cord wherever possible; the knowledge that he was going to marry Claudia and the facts she had learnt about his past the night before had muddled her mind and confused her emotions to the point where there was just one giant ache where her brain should have been. She wanted to get home and be by herself to sort out how she felt and begin to cope with it.

It was just after seven when the fleet of taxis arrived to take everyone back. As Aline walked down the stairs with her overnight bag, Cord appeared from his study and called her name.

'Yes?' She looked at him warily; she had been counting the minutes till she could escape.

'I've just had a phone call from Hantine,' he informed her quietly. 'I need your help for a couple of hours if that is convenient? I will take you home immediately we've finished.'

She nodded in agreement as her heart sank. Was this weekend never going to end? She heard her name called from one of the waiting taxis and he frowned impatiently. 'Tell them to go.' He was his usual egotistical self and a small smile touched her mouth fleetingly. He had switched back into work mode and it was all business now.

It was over two hours later, when they were drawing to a close, that she raised her head to find his dark eyes on her face. 'Tired?' His voice was bland, but there was something in his face that pulled at her nerves. 'Go and freshen up and I'll pour us both a drink before we leave.'

She rose gratefully, stretching her slender body as she did so. It had been warm in the small study and she felt hot and sticky in the jumper and trousers she had been wearing all day. 'I won't be a minute.'

He nodded distractedly as he finished writing the last of the figures he had calculated, and as she passed through the hall she picked up her overnight bag on impulse, deciding to change into the spare jumper she had brought. She found the room she had shared with Wendy earlier, and after laying the clean jumper on her bed stripped off her sweater and bra thankfully. The cool night air felt wonderful on her overheated skin.

After sluicing down her top half quickly in the small basin in the bathroom and brushing her hair into ordered sleekness, she wandered out into the bedroom to get dressed again. She had just reached for her bra when she heard the firm, heavy footsteps on the landing outside, and before she could move Cord had swung open the door, talking as he did so. 'You must be hungry; there are all manner of goodies in the fridge...'

She froze under his startled glance as his voice died away, too surprised for a brief moment to cover herself, and then gave a little cry of embarrassment as she hugged her arms around her in an effort to cover her full breasts from his silent gaze.

'Talking of goodies...' He was trying to be flippant to save the situation, but deep red colour had suffused the paleness of her skin and he seemed unable to tear his eyes away from the sight of her nakedness. 'I'm sorry.' His voice was gruff. 'I thought you were just doing your hair; I didn't expect——'

She closed her eyes for an instant and when she opened them again there was a gentleness melting the hard face. 'You're very beautiful, Aline—there's nothing to be ashamed of.'

'It's not that...' She found she was stuttering and wished he would leave so that she could continue getting dressed.

'Is it me?' He took a step nearer and there was fire burning in his eyes. 'You don't want me to see you? But why? You're a woman and I'm a man; if anyone is going to appreciate all you have to offer, I will.'

'Please, Cord.' He moved even nearer, seeming to be drawn to her side in spite of himself, his breathing audible in the quiet room.

'Don't be frightened.' There was a thickness in the deep voice and his arms were tense as he pulled her into him. 'I don't want to hurt you; don't you know that?' His hands moved over her back caressingly as he held her to him, and she shivered helplessly at the touch of his fingers, warm and coaxing, on her skin.

'But you will, won't you?' Her voice was a whisper and he frowned as he looked down at her, passion turning his eyes into grey pools, his brown skin dark against her fairness.

'I will what?'

'Hurt me.' She raised her face to his as she spoke and her eyes were the soft, pleading eyes of a wounded doe before the hunter. 'You won't want to, but you will.'

He grew very still. 'Is that what you think of me?' There was deep hurt as well as anger in his voice and for a moment she was tempted to fall against him in surrender, but then the voice of cold reason spoke and she took a step backwards as his hands fell to his sides.

'But it's what you have told me yourself.' Her voice faltered as she looked at him. 'You don't want commitment, love, the normal things. Even this thing with Claudia—you don't really *love* her, do you?'

'You still believe there is such a thing as love?' His face was icy cold.

'Of course.' She reached for her sweater as she spoke and hugged it to her, glad of the diversion to hide her face for a moment. Did she believe in love? He would never know the irony of his words.

'What you are talking about is marriage, a money ticket.' The hooded eyes were chilly. 'A price a man pays.'

'It's not a price, not the way you think.' She could feel tears threatening to choke her words but desperately wanted him to understand. 'Real marriage has nothing to do with how much money you have or don't have. It's based on love, sharing the good and bad times together, looking after each other... I couldn't exist in a relationship that wasn't built on that.'

'You're talking make-believe.' He suddenly sounded immensely weary.

'No, look at Uncle Ron. He's been happily married for years, and my own parents loved each other till the day they died.'

'You can't be sure of that,' he said quietly.

'Well, your own parents, then?'

'That was different.' There was a stricken look in his eyes as he spoke. 'Theirs was the exception that proves the rule. What you are telling me is the age-old demand. If I want you I have to pay for it in marriage.'

'No, that's not what I'm telling you,' she said gently.

'No?' His mouth twisted bitterly. 'You're not being honest again. If I offered to marry you now, to make you secure with a bit of paper that isn't worth that much——' he clicked his long fingers scornfully '——you'd fall at my feet. No woman passes up an offer of unlimited wealth, with the security of a free meal-ticket for life if things go wrong.' His voice was blazingly arrogant.

'I would.' She looked him straight in the face. 'I can honestly say I wouldn't marry you if you were the last man on earth.' Because I couldn't live with you knowing you don't love me, my darling, she thought miserably. You would destroy me in weeks.

'I don't believe you.' His eyes bored into her face as though he would look into her mind. 'I don't believe you,' he repeated slowly, but she could see from the growing awareness in his face that he knew she was telling the truth, and his mouth straightened into a thin white line.

'If I made love to you now I could have you begging me to take you within five minutes.'

'You'd have to rape me first.'

'And you think I wouldn't?'

'I *know* you wouldn't.' She looked at him carefully. 'I might not know you very well, Cord, I doubt if there's anyone who does, but I would bank my life on the fact that you wouldn't inflict yourself where you weren't wanted.'

He stiffened and drew away from her as the fire died in his eyes. 'I have never heard such a magnificent insult wrapped in such pretty packaging.' He turned and walked to the door slowly. 'I won't bother you again, you have my word on that.'

'Cord——' For a moment she was going to tell him he didn't understand, that she loved him, would do anything for him. But then he turned and his face was the cold face of a stranger, with dead eyes which looked through her. It chilled her bones and froze the words forming on her lips, and she stared at him helplessly as the ice in his eyes dismissed her.

'We'll forgo the snack.' Even his voice sounded different. 'Be ready in five minutes. I'll wait in the car.'

She sank down on to the bed as he left, her whole body beginning to shake with reaction. How had it all happened? Her mind raced frantically and she groaned softly. There was nothing else she could have done or said. She couldn't let him know she loved him; even this pain was preferable to the agony she would have felt then. She rocked backwards and forwards on the bed with her arms tight round her body, seeking comfort that wasn't there.

The next few days were difficult and tense, and it grated unbearably on Aline that Cord seemed to show no sign of the anguish that was eating into her soul. True, he was a little colder than usual with his employees, accepting their thanks for the weekend with cool unsmiling nods and treating her with an icy formality that never cracked for a moment.

It was now just over a week since the barbecue, and Pierre Asvana was due to arrive that afternoon for a meeting with Cord. Aline hoped his daughter wouldn't accompany him; she hadn't seen Claudia since that night in Cord's garden and was dreading any confrontation the lovely redhead might provoke.

It was late afternoon when she heard voices outside her door and with a sinking heart she recognised the sharp click of Claudia's unmistakable footsteps just a moment before she entered with her father. The older woman's face was cold and her blank stare warned Aline to keep a low profile, but she was surprised by Pierre Asvana's attitude. He normally stopped for a few minutes by her desk to exchange pleasantries, but this afternoon he swept by her as though she didn't exist, entering Cord's office with Claudia a step behind before Aline could even buzz.

Aline let a small sigh of relief escape her lips as the door clicked shut. She felt like a bird with a broken wing at the moment, and Claudia would be quick to seize upon any display of weakness.

Within minutes she heard raised voices from the inner room, which faded quickly, only to swell in volume seconds later. She recognised Cord's voice with a feeling of surprise; she had never known him to shout in all the time she had worked for him. He had a reputation for remaining cool in any circumstances. She glanced nervously at the closed door; it sounded like a war breaking out in there. Whatever was wrong? She wasn't left to speculate much longer. The door was suddenly jerked open and Cord stood in the doorway, his handsome face black with rage and his grey eyes as cold as ice.

'Would you come into my office for a moment, please, Aline?' His voice belied the fury that was turning his countenance dark; it was cool and firm without a tremor.

She followed him into the room apprehensively, her eyes flicking to the other two occupants, who were staring straight ahead. Just for a split-second Claudia allowed her gaze to shift and meet Aline's eyes, and there was cold poison in the slanted eyes.

'It seems we have a problem.' Cord's face was a tight mask, his eyes shadowed so that she could read nothing in their grey depths.

'Yes?' She looked directly at Cord as she spoke, trying to concentrate on him and him alone. 'Can I help?'

Claudia gave a small, sharp explosion of a laugh. 'Help?' Her lips drew back from her small white teeth in a curling sneer that distorted the lovely face into a mocking caricature. 'I think you've done enough.'

'Claudia!' Her father's voice was a pistol shot. 'Let Cord handle this.'

'Aline.' Cord leant forward across his desk towards her as he spoke, totally ignoring the other two. 'Do you remember some papers I asked you to work on for me a few weeks ago relating to the financial considerations of the merger? They involved the interests of several of our suppliers and were very detailed.'

'I'm not sure.' She wrinkled her brow as she tried to think. 'There have been so many reports and letters to translate.'

'Think hard; it's very important.' Cord's voice was urgent as he looked into her clear gaze.

'Oh, this is absolutely pathetic.' Claudia moved restlessly in her seat, crossing and uncrossing her long, slim legs. 'What are we going all through this for? It's perfectly obvious, isn't it? For goodness' sake——'

'One more word and I shall personally escort you out of this building. Have I made myself clear?' Cord had turned to Claudia so savagely that she had jumped, and now angry red colour flared up her neck and into the high feline cheekbones. She cast a tight appealing glance at her father but he was still staring straight ahead, his face set and stony.

'I think I know the ones you mean.' Cord's eyes turned back to fasten on Aline's pale face when she spoke. 'We kept them locked in the safe unless we were actually working on them?'

'Yes.' He relaxed slightly. 'There were only two copies of all the documents; I had one set and Pierre the other. We both thought we had taken all the necessary precautions to preserve their confidentiality but now it appears a rival company has laid their hands on a set. Fortunately I know the managing director very well, and when one of his minions brought him such a scoop he phoned me immediately to put me in the picture, which in the circumstances was extremely generous. It means the whole deal is now on the open market if our competitor feels like making those documents public. It would cause unnecessary panic, and Pierre and I could lose a considerable amount of money.'

'I see,' said Aline slowly, although nothing was further from the truth. 'How can I help?'

'By telling us the name of your contact and how much they were commissioned to pay you.' Claudia's glittering eyes were full of malignant hostility.

'That's enough!' Cord leapt to his feet and was round the desk in an instant. 'I warned you, Claudia.'

'Please, Cord.' Pierre Asvana had also risen and placed a tired hand on his friend's shoulder. 'This has been a great shock for us all; no more fighting, please. Can't we discuss this like reasonable adults? I'm not accusing anyone at this time.'

'I am!' Claudia intended to have her pound of flesh.

'You think I sold these papers to someone?' Aline's face was white with shock and anger as she looked Cord full in the face. 'Is that what this is all about?'

She heard him take a long deep breath before he replied, and then his voice was cool and gentle. 'No one is accusing you, Aline. There is no proof whatsoever. Unfortunately there are only the four of us who had access to the documents at any time as far as we know, and that is why I had to ask you if you knew anything I didn't. Perhaps someone came in when you were working on them? You left them overnight on your desk by accident? Anything like that?'

'No.' She didn't take her eyes off his face. 'I always locked them away again. I still have the spare safe key.'

'Yes, I know.' He looked at her quietly.

'You have a key?' Claudia almost screeched the words, and there was immense satisfaction in her flushed face that wasn't lost on anyone present. 'Well, that's it, then! You didn't tell us she had a key.' She glared balefully at Cord.

'It was none of your business,' he said stonily.

'None of my business?' she repeated spitefully. 'Oh, wonderful, wonderful! The great Cord Lachoni falls for the tricks of a little bit of a secretary and is taken for the ride of the century! I can't wait till they find out about this. You're going to be the laughing-stock to end them all, darling. Your credibility is going to be nil, stone-cold zero!'

'It was a mistake to bring you.' Pierre Asvana's quiet voice brought the vindictive tirade to an abrupt halt. He had a grey tinge to his face and his eyes were cloudy as he looked at his only daughter, and something in the thin, lined face caused Claudia to put her hand to her mouth.

'I'm sorry, Daddy.' She put out a hand to him but he pushed it aside and turned to Cord slowly.

'I apologise for this travesty of a meeting, Cord. I had thought we could get to the bottom of this thing, but maybe it isn't that simple. You'll make enquiries?' Cord nodded slowly. 'I'll be at home if you need me.'

He walked from the office, slightly hunched as though in pain, with Claudia trailing silently behind him. Cord watched them go with an expression of deep concern twisting his face, and as the sound of their footsteps faded he turned back to Aline, who was still sitting, frozen with shock, in her chair.

'I'll need to investigate, you understand?' She nodded numbly. 'There's nothing you want to tell me, nothing you've forgotten?'

She stared at him as the blood chilled in her veins and the hairs on the back of her neck stood up. 'You think it was me, don't you?' She rose in her seat until she was standing in front of him, her face as white as a sheet and her eyes huge with hurt. 'You believe every word Claudia said!' She was shouting at him now.

'Calm yourself.' He looked at her coldly. 'You're becoming hysterical.'

'Hysterical!' She knew this wouldn't convince that hard, analytical mind, but suddenly all the accumulated pain of weeks was pouring out in a furious torrent she couldn't have stopped if she had wanted to. 'You were just waiting for something to prove you right, weren't you? Anything would do! Forget whether it's true or not!' His dark face froze. 'Well, I'm not going to stay here to be interrogated by you or anyone else! You can stuff your precious job, Cord Lachoni. I quit!'

She was across the room and into her office in an instant, her cheeks burning scarlet and a buzzing in her ears that was deafening her. She saw that the door leading into the main office was open and everyone had stopped working, the silence complete.

Cord followed her to her desk, kicking the door shut savagely as he glared ferociously at his goggle-eyed employees. 'What do you think you're doing?'

She was throwing the few personal items on her desk into her bag with jerky, uncontrolled movements, her whole body shaking as though she were on strings.

'What does it look like?' She almost spat the words into his face and for a second he looked as though he was going to strike her, so great was his fury.

'It looks as if you've gone stark, staring mad!' He was shouting now, and in the midst of her pain she knew a moment's deep satisfaction that for once he wasn't fully in control. 'I'm the one who should be throwing a blue fit, not you!'

'Oh, go to hell!' She was beyond fear or rational thought. She had never felt so utterly enraged in all her life. 'It's been nothing but misery since the day I met you and I've had enough! More than enough! I didn't take your stupid papers that interfered with your little power games, but I wish I had. Anything to throw a spanner into the works of the great human machine, Cord Lachoni!' Her eyes were blazing with such fury that for a moment he was speechless. 'You've called me a cheat and a fraud, you've never believed a word I've said——' She was round the desk and had opened the door before he had time to move, and as she strode away down the outer office he went to follow her, stopping abruptly in the doorway as he noticed the incredulous shocked faces of his workforce. He froze for a moment and then turned back towards his office, slamming the door shut with such savagery that a piece of plaster dislodged itself from the ceiling and fell with a crash on the floor.

CHAPTER NINE

ALINE never could remember how she reached her apartment; the walk remained a blank forever in her mind. She was trembling so much that it took her an age to get the key in the lock, and she fell into the quiet, sunlit room as the door swung open. She looked around in stunned silence. The same stereotyped pictures hung on the walls, the breakfast dishes were still waiting to be washed—it was all just as she had left it this morning. Her world had been blown into a million tiny pieces and yet there was nothing to show for it.

She phoned the airport before she even took her coat off. 'Yes, Miss Marcell, we can fit you in on a flight tomorrow morning.' The well-spoken voice at the other end of the phone was clinically helpful. 'You will need to be at the airport to check in at ten o'clock. OK? Fine. Have a good flight.'

She lost two hours sitting in a trance in the chair as the afternoon darkened into dusk and the blue shadows of evening encroached into the room. She was brought out of her reverie by a sharp knock at the door. She opened it, still in a daze, to find Cord's large shape filling the doorway, his face harsh.

'I don't want to talk to you.' Her voice was faint and she didn't open the door any wider.

'Nevertheless, we *are* going to talk,' he said grimly, his eyes sweeping over her white face intently. 'We can do it here in the corridor or in your apartment.'

She hesitated for a moment and he pushed the door aside as he walked past her, turning to face her as he reached the centre of the room, his arms crossed and his long, muscled legs slightly astride. 'Are you going to be sensible or are we still playing amateur dramatics?'

'If by that you are asking whether I'm going to come back to work for you, the answer is no.' She was glad of the anaesthetising numbness that had coated her mind; she found she was quite unaffected by his furious stare.

'I don't think you are in any position to make up your own mind about that,' he said coldly, his voice soft with warning. 'There are more than just your interests at stake, surely?'

'You mean Tim?' She looked at him with wide, clear eyes. 'I'm not responsible for my brother any more, Mr Lachoni.' His face tightened as she said his name, but the steel-grey eyes didn't flicker. 'The reason I'm in this mess now is because of him, and for the first time since all this began I can see things clearly. I'm not doing him any favours by wrapping him up in cotton wool. It's time he faced up to the consequences of his own actions.'

'And your actions? Are you prepared to face a court and admit your part in the thing?'

'The first time I knew anything about the embezzlement was when you spoke to me in the office that night.' She stared at him fiercely. 'Jennie and her husband repaid the money I had lent her years ago and I used that for my holiday. I have no fear about facing a court because by the time that happens I will have been able to contact Jennie and ask her to confirm what I've told you. I didn't see a penny of your money. Believe it or not. I don't really care.'

'You're asking me to believe that you would tie yourself to me for a year in order for your brother to remain free? That you have no fear for yourself?'

'I'm not asking you to believe anything,' she said coolly. 'I'm finished with all that. I can prove what I've said and that's all that matters now.'

'And this latest catastrophe? Don't you think that by running away you will be admitting guilt?' he asked quietly.

'I'm not guilty.' She raised her head proudly. '*I* know it, and the rest of you can go to blazes.'

'That's twice you've told me where I can go today, and neither time was it a destination I would choose,' he said thoughtfully, his accent more pronounced than usual. 'What makes you think I agree with Claudia?'

'I don't care if you agree with her or not,' she said coldly. 'You certainly didn't disagree, if I remember rightly. You let her accuse me without a word in my defence.'

'That's not quite true.'

'I'm leaving tomorrow morning anyway. I've booked the flight and I shall be home in England by evening.' Her voice cracked slightly as she spoke. She suddenly had a wildly intense longing to see Tim and her uncle and be on home soil.

'I won't allow it!'

'*You* won't allow it! You have no say in the matter. You are nothing to me.' She lowered her gaze as she lied.

'So you have made clear in the past,' he said grimly. 'Be warned, Aline, I won't go back on my word. I will see you and Tim in court first.'

'So be it.' Now she knew how a broken heart felt.

'Look, stop this.' He took a step towards her, his eyes suddenly the eyes of a much younger Cord. 'Don't go like this; don't make me fight you.'

'I can't stay.' How can I, she asked him silently, loving you the way I do?

'Please, Aline.' She had the impression the plea was foreign to his lips, and in spite of everything hope flared briefly.

'Why do you want me to stay?' she asked slowly.

He stared at her silently for a full minute, his eyes locked in some violent inner battle that showed in the tenseness of the square jaw and straight mouth, and then he shook his head despairingly.

'Isn't it enough that I have asked you?'

'No, it's not enough.' Her voice was a cry for understanding.

'I can't change.' There was a touch of arrogance in his voice now that strengthened her resolve. 'I am what I am. I take what I want until I'm tired of it; all men do. I'm just more honest than most.'

'You didn't take me.' She hadn't meant to say the words, they had just slipped out, but it was almost as though she had insulted him, reminded him of a weakness he was trying to forget.

'Maybe that was a mistake,' he said softly. 'Perhaps I should have had you that night, regardless of your innocence. What would it matter if you hated me in the morning? You do anyway.'

'I don't hate you.'

He pulled her towards him abruptly. 'I'm sick of words. You are just like any other woman; there is only one thing you really understand.' His lips covered hers in angry possession as the weight of his powerful body forced her against the wall, rendering her helpless and leaving his hands free to trace a burning path over her softness. 'I won't allow you to leave me; you are mine until I say differently.'

The kiss was deep and long and sensual, his tongue plundering her mouth until she was trembling against him while his hands worked their subtle magic on her body. 'If nothing else, I can make you want me, can't I?' She was melting into him, the trauma and exhaustion of the day forgotten in the thrilling sensation of being held close to his hard body. 'Say you are mine—say it.'

Having to think forced her mind back into some semblance of reality, and as she stiffened and tried to move out of his arms he increased his lovemaking to the point where she began to think she would faint if his hands and mouth didn't stop their sensual work. 'Cord...'

His breathing was harsh and uneven when at last he pulled himself away to stand looking down at her, a strange, tormented darkness in his face. 'There's so much more if you would only give yourself freely to me. I want you, Aline. I'm eating, sleeping, breathing you. It's driving me mad. Tell me another man could make you feel the way I do. We could be good together, you know we could.'

She couldn't answer at first, but as her breathing steadied and the mad pounding of her heart began to die down she looked up into his waiting face with sad eyes. 'I've never doubted for a minute that we'd be good together.' As a light flashed across his face she put out a hand warningly. 'But it's not enough, is it? Not for me. How long would it last? One year, two maybe, but without love the craving would begin to go sour and desire would fade. I'm a novelty to you at the moment, a new toy.' He went to reply but she checked him with a shake of her head. 'It's true, Cord—look into your heart.'

'I know what's in my heart.' His voice was rough.

'And I know what's in mine. I can't be what you want me to be. There are hundreds of girls out there who would jump at the chance to be in your bed, but I'm not one of them.'

'What if I said I'd marry you—what then?' His eyes were boring into hers and she quelled the sudden throb of excitement his words provoked before it showed on her face.

'Even if you did, it wouldn't make any difference. You don't understand, do you? You really don't see. We don't love each other, and sex wouldn't be enough for me; ultimately it wouldn't for you.'

'You're chasing a rainbow, Aline.' He walked across the room away from her as he spoke, and his face was drained of colour. 'Some elusive emotion, when the real thing is staring you in the face. Love is the animal mating of two bodies; it begins and ends with that. Writers and poets might fantasise, but it's sexual compatibility that counts. We have that, I know it.'

'Is that what you had with Megan?' She had to ask. It was crazy to be jealous of something that had finished all those years ago, but she was. She was the only woman he had married, after all.

'She didn't make the earth move, if that's what you mean.' His eyes were bitter. 'I have the feeling you could, but we shall never know, shall we? Why does it have to be forever with you? Why can't you just live for today?'

'Because there are a lot of tomorrows,' she said quietly.

'Are you determined to go?'

'Yes.' She faced him squarely. 'I have to.'

'How are you getting to the airport tomorrow?'

'What?' She stared at him in surprise. The change of direction had thrown her momentarily. 'Oh—by taxi. I've already ordered it.'

'Cancel it.' His voice was brusque.

'Look, I thought we'd just agreed——'

'We haven't agreed anything, but I don't mean that you shouldn't go. If you insist on committing vocational suicide and taking Tim with you that's your business, but I won't have any one of my employees struggling to the airport in a foreign country and paying for the privilege. I'll come and pick you up. What time is your flight?'

She told him wonderingly. She couldn't make him out. He was a total mystery.

'I shall get to the bottom of this farce over the document, Aline.' She couldn't ascertain from the cold voice whether it was a threat or a promise. 'And I will be in touch. I think you are making a grave mistake in leaving before the matter is settled, but if you're determined...?' She nodded slowly. He gave her one last long look and then left quietly, leaving her more puzzled and heartsore than ever.

True to his word, he arrived with time to spare the next day. Her heart stopped and then raced jerkily as she answered his hard knock, to find him leaning lazily against the wall outside, his face cold and still and his eyes hooded. 'All ready?' His voice was casual, even nonchalant; he had clearly mastered his strange animal passion for her and was prepared to face the inevitable with none of the overwhelming misery that had kept Aline awake most of the night.

Her eyes wanted to feast on him, to take in every detail of his hard, dark face. This was probably the last time she would see him, unless he made a personal appearance in the threatened court case, but he brushed past her, picking up the cases and moving outside on to the landing again. 'Your key?' She handed it to him silently, and he locked the door and then slipped the key into his pocket.

'I was going to give it to the concierge as I left.'

He looked at her with unfathomable eyes. 'That won't be necessary; I will see to 'it.'

It was raining a little as they left the apartment block, and the air smelt fresh and clean, with the taste of autumn in its coolness. 'There'll be no leaves on the trees when I get home.' She spoke her thoughts out loud as she gazed round one last time at the familiar street.

'I suppose not.' There was a severity in his gaze that hurt her, but perhaps it was better than the hot desire of the night before.

She sat in the car as he loaded the cases in the boot. She would have given anything for the numbness of the day before to take over her senses, but there was no such relief today. Everything was bright and crystal-clear, with a sharpness that was painful.

As they drew into the large car park at the airport the last faint hope that she had been unwittingly nurturing died in her breast. She realised in that instant that she had been secretly hoping for a reprieve, unable to believe that he would let her leave him for good, waiting to hear him say it was all a mistake with Claudia and that he loved her, Aline, that he couldn't live without her... She smiled to herself with bitter self-mockery.

'You had better put this in your bag.' He had called a porter to take care of her cases and was standing quietly by the side of the car as she looked at him with blank eyes.

'What is it?' She looked at the envelope he was offering.

'Your plane fare, with a little left over until you get another job.'

Aline turned startled eyes up to the dark face. 'That's not necessary. Please, I don't want it.'

'Don't be obstinate. You have earned every penny. It was in our agreement that I would pay for your ticket both ways and you have more than earned the little that is in there.'

'I don't understand you at all.' She put one small hand on his broad chest and he looked down at its smoothness, his face constricting suddenly.

'That makes two of us, Aline. Goodbye.' He made no attempt to kiss her, sliding swiftly into the car and pulling away immediately in a screech of burning tyres. He had gone! Left her, just like that, with no kind words to soften the blow. She felt drunk with pain, swaying slightly in the cool air as she stared after the car until it was lost in the misty drizzle.

'Aline! Over here!' As she walked out of Customs weighed down with her cases she was amazed to see her uncle and Tim standing to one side of the milling crowd.

'What are you doing here?' She knew she was going to cry; it was welling up inside like a dam that was about to break.

'Cord phoned me last night.' Her uncle took one case and Tim grasped the other two as they drew her out of the path of the returning passengers before stopping and giving her two huge bear-hugs. 'He said there had been some unpleasantness and you were very distressed. He didn't want you getting off the plane with no one to meet you.'

That did it! As she collapsed against them the dam burst, water flooding from her eyes and filling her mouth and ears with agonised weeping. 'Aline, darling...' She wasn't aware that they were walking but within minutes she found herself seated in the small coffee-lounge with the two men patting her hands and tut-tutting in the way men did when they were completely at a loss as to how to handle a woman's tears.

'I'm sorry...' It was a good five minutes later before she was able to control the gasping sobs that were shaking her body, but in the midst of all the painful weeping something had been released and she felt slightly more at peace.

Over coffee she related the events of the last twenty-four hours which had culminated in her departure from France, and her uncle looked at her in bewilderment as she finished speaking. 'But what makes you think Cord suspects you? He said nothing to suggest that when he phoned.' He looked at her strangely. 'There's something you aren't telling me, my girl, and from Tim's face he's got a good idea what this is all about.'

Tim glanced at her and then turned to his uncle, a sheepish expression turning his brown eyes mournful. 'It's all down to me really, Uncle Ron. Mr Lachoni has always believed that Aline was involved in the embezzlement.'

'What?' Her uncle turned to her with a deep frown. 'Didn't you tell him you had nothing to do with it?'

'Of course I did.' Aline rubbed her hand over her hot, sticky face wearily. 'It didn't make any difference; he had made up his mind right from the beginning and that was it. I don't suppose you can blame him really; it——'

'I certainly can blame him!' Her uncle was livid, his lined face turning a dark shade of red. 'I thought Cord had more sense! Then...' He stopped and wrinkled his brow and Aline had a good idea of what was coming next. 'The job? Why did he give you such a good job? I don't understand any of this.'

'The job was a form of punishment.' Tim's voice was flat. 'You know my penance—well, it was Aline who really got the short straw. She had to go and work for him for a year out there with hardly any pay and doing whatever hours he cared to demand, and——'

'It wasn't as bad as that,' Aline said quickly, not liking the picture her brother was painting of Cord. 'He was very good to me, as it happens. I had a nice apartment and the work was interesting. It was Claudia who made things difficult.'

'I remember Miss Asvana from way back,' her uncle said thoughtfully. 'They had something going once a long time ago, but when it ended she hounded Cord for months; it got thoroughly embarrassing. It's a shame, because he thinks a lot of her father.'

'Well, I think whatever it was they had has been resurrected,' said Aline stiffly.

'What?' Her uncle looked at her keenly until she turned away as a warm flush invaded her cheeks. 'Oh, Aline.' His voice was soft with understanding. 'Now I see.'

'What do you see?' Tim looked from one to the other, sensing there was something vital he had missed. 'What's the matter...?' His voice trailed away as he looked deep into his twin's eyes. 'Oh, you great twit.' His voice was flat but not unsympathetic. 'To fall for him of all people—you must want your head examining.'

'Shut up, Tim.' Understanding they might be, but Aline suddenly found she couldn't take the sympathy. 'I don't want to talk about it. I'm going to take a break somewhere for a few days and get myself sorted out. Is that OK?' She looked at her uncle.

He nodded slowly. 'Of course; you're a grown woman used to making decisions. How are you for cash?'

'Fine.' She couldn't stop the tell-tale flush staining her pale cheeks again. 'Cord bought the ticket home and gave me some extra; I didn't realise how much until I was on the plane. I'll pay him back when I get a job.'

Her uncle shook his head slowly. 'Well, well. This isn't the Cord I know at all. This whole thing has amazed me.' He looked at his niece's soft dark brown eyes and the mass of silky blonde hair, and his eyes narrowed thoughtfully. 'But perhaps it shouldn't have. Everyone meets their Waterloo at some stage.'

'What?' Aline had lost the thread of the conversation and he smiled at her blank face.

'Nothing, child, nothing.' He patted her hand. 'Let's go home. You are staying with us overnight and then we'll see about that holiday.'

It was early the next morning when she heard the phone ringing in the small square hall of her uncle's house. She hadn't slept well, skimming in and out of confused nightmarish dreams, her mind searching for rest in the shadowed world of the subconscious.

'Aline.' Her uncle's voice sounded outside the door as he knocked gently.

'Yes?' She sat up quickly in the small narrow bed.

'Cord's on the phone. He wants to speak to you. I told him *you* might not want to talk to him!'

'No, it's all right.' Her heart was thumping so hard that it was hurting her chest. 'It might be important; I'd better speak to him.'

She pulled on her robe and slid her feet into warm slippers, patting her uncle's concerned face as she passed him on the landing and descending the wide carpeted stairs on shaking legs. She picked up the phone nervously. 'Hello?'

'Aline? How are you?' As that familiar deep voice sounded down the wire she felt her knees begin to tremble and sat down hastily on the carpet.

'I'm fine.' She waited for him to speak, her palms wet and her mouth dry.

'I'm sorry to call so early, but there was something I had to tell you,' he said quietly. The dark voice was giving nothing away; she couldn't tell how he was feeling.

'Yes?'

'It isn't very pleasant, I'm afraid.'

Her stomach lurched and she waited in trepidation. What now?

'Pierre Asvana had a massive heart attack during the night and isn't expected to live.'

'Oh, no.' She stared uncomprehendingly at the plastic in her hand. 'Poor man.'

'Quite.' His voice was almost expressionless as though he was exerting iron control. 'It was clearly brought on by the worry of the last few days. I had a word with Claudia at the hospital. She is most distraught. If she is capable of loving anyone I think it is probably him.'

She waited. He was leading up to something; she knew the signs.

'Claudia confirmed what I had already suspected: that she was responsible for the leaked papers and so on.'

'Claudia?' Aline's voice was a faint disbelieving squeak but he still heard it, and his cold, modulated tones sounded down the line.

'Of course. It was obvious, wasn't it? I knew I hadn't done it and clearly Pierre wouldn't; that only left Claudia.'

'There was me.' Her voice was small.

'Don't be ridiculous.' His voice had that tinge of male arrogance that had so annoyed her in the early days. 'That was never a possibility as far as I was concerned.'

'Wasn't it?' Her head was swimming.

'Of course not. I know you better than that.' There was a pregnant silence and she couldn't break it. She was shaking so much that she thought she would be sick at any moment.

'So. . .' He paused as though he found it difficult to go on. 'You can come back. Have a few days with Ronald and then——'

'I'm not coming back to France, Cord.' The nausea had gone and she leaned back against the wall gratefully.

'Of course you are.' He sounded very patronising, and for a moment she almost smiled as she pictured his hard, frowning face at the other end of the phone. 'I told you, Claudia has admitted her guilt. It appears her motive was to discredit you, and the loss of thousands of pounds wasn't even a consideration.' His voice was dry. 'I'll explain it all when you get back; I need to see you face to face.'

'I understand what you're saying.' She tried to keep the tremors that were shaking her from coming through in her voice. 'But I'm not coming back. I can't.'

'Of course you can,' he said irritably. 'There's no reason——'

'There is a reason and I'm not coming.' She took a deep breath. 'Do your worst, Cord, but I am *not coming back*.' She spaced the words out slowly and there was no mistaking the rigid determination in her voice. There was absolute quiet and then his voice sounded again, different now.

'I need you here, Aline—the work and so on...' He stopped and cleared his throat. 'You will come back; I'll make you.'

'You can't bully me any more, Cord.' She was fighting back the tears but they must have showed in her voice because his was suddenly hoarse.

'Don't cry. You aren't crying, are you? Listen——'

'I can't come back and I never want to see you again. Is that clear enough for you? I can't take any more; you're killing me with your hot and cold and Claudia and everything...' Her voice was rising in pitch. 'I can't carry on working with you every day, feeling the way I do. I can't be the sort of woman you want, and you've made it plain how you feel about me.'

'Aline——'

'No, I don't want to hear it all again!' Her voice was wild now and the tears were raining down her face. 'They're just empty words, as you are empty inside. I wish I'd never met you! I love you, but I wish I'd never met you!' She banged the receiver down on his voice and turned to her uncle who had shot down the stairs and was standing grim-faced by her side.

'I've got to get away, Uncle.' She stared at him desperately and he nodded slowly.

'Yes, I can see that.' The phone started ringing again and she clutched at his arm pleadingly.

'Don't answer it, please don't answer it.'

'I didn't intend to.' He put his arm round her shoulders and hugged her gently. 'Now go and have a shower and get dressed while I make a pot of coffee. We'll have a word with your aunt and see if you can borrow her car for a few days. OK?' She nodded wanly. 'This will pass, my pet.' His voice was gentle. 'I had a disastrous love-affair years ago before I met your aunt and I thought my world had come to an end. But then I slowly got better and...' He shrugged. 'Life goes on.'

He was trying to be kind, but he didn't understand. She knew with a dreadful certainty that she would never marry now, never have children and a mate to call her very own. If she couldn't have Cord, then she didn't want anyone.

She looked back afterwards on the next few days as though they were a time-warp. She had taken off later that same morning in her aunt's small white car, not knowing where she was going or for how long, but with an aching desire to be alone, without the need to talk or think.

She drove for miles in the cold November air, stopping for lunch at a small wayside pub and then continuing

on her journey as her exhausted mind slowly relaxed in
the peace and quiet of the surrounding countryside.

It was late evening when she reached a small village
in the heart of Yorkshire, rimmed in by low hills and
drifting clouds, where the air smelt of burning logs and
the pace of life was immeasurably slow. She checked into
the tiny inn, pleased to find that she was the only guest
staying so late in the season, and after a good supper of
home-cooked steak and kidney pie washed down with
two glasses of real ale she went up to her small room
under the eaves and slept deeply and well till morning.

The weather was cold but dry and she went walking
each day, a rucksack that the kindly landlady had given
her on her back, carrying her packed lunch and a book,
spending hours in the rolling green countryside where
crystal-clear streams splashed over age-old rocks and tiny,
exquisite, sparkling waterfalls were behind every corner.
She returned each evening as the sweet smell of
woodsmoke drifted on the cold air and dusk cast its grey
shadows over the small village, eating the country fare
that the landlady put before her with hungry appreci-
ation and falling into the small bed too physically
exhausted even to brush her teeth.

It was the afternoon of the seventh day, as she stood
listening to the pure notes of a missel thrush on a high
bank that overlooked the village, that she became aware
that someone had walked up from the inn in the distance
and was standing close by, watching her. She turned
slowly, the hairs on the back of her neck rising, and
knew a moment of blind animal panic as her wide eyes
fastened on Cord standing leaning lazily against the
massive trunk of an old oak tree.

'No!' Whatever he had expected, it wasn't the spitting
fury who backed away from him as though he were the

devil himself and disappeared down the other side of the hill at a fast gallop.

'Aline!' She was deaf to his voice as she raced down the woodland path at the bottom of the hill, and it wasn't until he caught her arm and swung her round so violently that they both overbalanced that some measure of sanity returned.

'Please, Aline, listen to me.' He was panting as he lay in the tufted grass to the side of the path, and she raised herself into a tight little ball, sitting with her arms round her knees as she put a few inches between them.

'How did you find me?'

He looked at her warily, clearly expecting her to take off again at any moment. 'I bribed Tim,' he said unselfconsciously.

'Bribed him?'

'I promised that if he told me where you were I'd consider the money matter closed. I think he's learnt his lesson anyway; I never intended to keep him to the four-year contract.'

She had felt it was a mistake to tell anyone where she was, but her uncle had been insistent that she keep in touch, and now, as she looked at Cord's dark face, she knew why. 'What do you want?'

'You.' His voice was thick, and the intensity of the grey eyes was frightening her.

'Keep away from me.' She backed a few more inches on her bottom but he didn't move, lying back in the green grass and surveying her tightly through narrowed hungry eyes.

'You can't get away from me. I won't let you.' His tone was quiet now but far from reassuring.

'Why have you come?' Her voice was weary and flat. 'Why can't you leave me alone?'

He moved restlessly. 'That's the question I had to ask myself, and do you know the conclusion I came up with?'

Aline shook her head silently, the sparkle of tears glimmering on her long thick eyelashes.

'Because I can't live without you.'

She shot to her feet, surprising both him and herself this time. 'Don't.' She shook her head desperately. 'Don't do this to me. I won't be any man's plaything.'

'Who said anything about a plaything?' He had risen slowly as he spoke and now he towered over her, his face fierce, but still making no attempt to touch her.

'Well, whatever you want to call it.' She forced the tears from her voice. 'You're going to marry Claudia——'

'Like hell I am!' It was the old Cord who was speaking, his face implacable and his eyes pure steel.

'But you said——'

'I never said anything; it was *you* who told *me*, if you remember. You didn't really believe that nonsense, did you, not when you had had time to think about it? What on earth do you think I am, a complete fool?'

'I have no idea what you are,' she said honestly as she felt her grasp on the situation diminishing rapidly.

'Look at me,' he said softly, an expression of tenderness replacing the hardness. 'What do you see?'

'I don't know...' Her voice was a whimper and he ran his hand through his black hair, making it stand up on end.

'For crying out loud, woman,' he said softly, 'you're not making this any easier. Look, sit down.' He waved his hand at the grass, and as she still didn't move his voice became a bark. 'Sit down!' She sank to the floor and he sat down carefully by her side, his eyes staring straight ahead. 'I want you to listen to what I have to say without moving or talking until I have finished. Will you do that?' There was a surprising note of pleading in his voice which she had never heard before, and it had her nodding her head in bemused silence.

'I think I knew almost from when we arrived in France that you weren't capable of stealing that money.' Her eyes widened with shock and he glanced at her before looking straight ahead again. 'I know, I know, I'm a first-class swine, but you attracted me, you see. I liked the packaging and I wanted to see more of the goods. I figured Tim owed me and I intended to make sure you wouldn't lose by it—a generous lump sum at the end of your time with me. I'd got it all worked out.' He paused. 'Then I got to know you better.'

He stood up, walking over to the small copse at the other side of the path and looking into the dense under-growth with his back to her. 'You made me realise that every preconceived idea I'd had about you was wrong. I couldn't believe it when I found out you were a virgin; the sort of women I'd got used to...' His voice hard-ened. 'Well, you've seen an example in Claudia. It isn't pretty, is it?' He sighed painfully. 'It was all too good to be true, but then came the sting in the tail. I dis-covered that, although I wanted you in my bed—needed you—I had to keep you at arm's length. For the first time in my life I was running away from something and I didn't like it. It made me angry. I couldn't handle it.'

He dug his hands deep into his pockets. 'When I thought you and Simon...' He shook his head slowly. 'I wanted to kill him, I mean *really* kill him.' The hard voice held a note of surprise. 'It showed me that the emotion I'd had for Megan hadn't been love. She hurt my pride at the time, but the main feeling I experienced when I threw her out was one of relief, coupled with the resolution that no woman would ever do that to me again. She'd sworn undying love from the first night we met, when all the time...' He waved his hand slowly. 'Anyway, that's all in the past, and that's where it's going to stay from now on.'

He paused. 'Taking you to the airport was the hardest thing I've ever done in my life.' He swung round as he growled the words and she saw the pain etched in his mouth. 'I knew I loved you but I couldn't admit it. No, that's not true. I dared not admit it.'

'No.' She shook her head in disbelief as she whispered the denial and he smiled humourlessly.

'You want to know the sort of state you'd reduced me to? I kept the key to your apartment so I could go and sit there close to where you'd been, smelling the perfume you wore, feeling you around. I sat there for hours, just thinking... Crazy, eh?' His mouth twisted. 'The invincible Cord Lachoni, head over heels in love with a little English schoolteacher who wouldn't give him the time of day.'

'It wasn't like that,' she whispered.

'It seemed like it. I'd have given the world for you to love me the way you described love, and yet part of me was glad you didn't. It was too much responsibility, too much potential heartache.' He smiled bitterly. 'I could still think like that when you were with me, but then you were gone. I had to face the fact that I'd lost you, that someone else would have the right to hold you, make you love him.' He paused. 'I wouldn't want my worst enemy to go through what I went through then. You were out in the world, breathing and living, and living a life in which I had no part.'

'Why didn't you tell me all this when you phoned, if it's true?' She dared not believe him, couldn't let herself hope.

'Because I'm a coward.' His eyes were anguished. 'It wasn't very pleasant facing that, either. I was going to get you back *my* way, make you come back and work for me and then court you, woo you, use every trick in the book if I had to. But get you back I was going to.' He groaned softly as he moved to stand in front of her. 'And then you told me you loved me. You had more courage in your little finger than I had in the whole of my body. It was like a punch in the guts, and then the phone went dead.'

'But Claudia?' She had to ask now in these moments of truth. 'You spent so much time with her.'

'Did I?' He looked surprised and then his face cleared. 'Not really; I spent a lot of time with Pierre and she was around, that's all. The little we'd had was finished with a long, long time ago and she knew the score. The spite with the papers was because I sent her packing on the night of the barbecue when I heard what she'd been telling you. I was less than tactful.'

He put out his hand to pull her up and she hesitated for a long moment. 'Aline...please.' There was a pain in his eyes that she recognised in her own heart. 'If you want revenge, you've had it in full this week, when I got over here and found you gone... It was days before I could force Ronald and Tim to talk; I nearly went insane.'

She put her small white hand in his large brown one and he pulled her gently to her feet. 'Pierre?' she asked stiffly.

'Damn Pierre!' He shook his head. 'I'm sorry—he's OK, he'll pull through. Aline——' He pulled her carefully towards him as though she were made of glass. 'I don't care about Pierre, I don't care about Tim or your uncle; the rest of the world doesn't exist any more. Talk to me, for pity's sake, tell me what you're feeling, if there's any hope for us.' She was frozen in his arms, terrified to give in to the feeling growing inside her. He stiffened as he looked down at her in his arms. 'I won't give up, you know. If I've killed your love for me I shall make it flower again. I want you and I won't let you go.' His accent was very pronounced, his eyes black with desire.

'Like your father,' she whispered faintly.

'Just like my father,' he agreed softly. 'For the first time in my life I know exactly what he felt when he looked at *his* little English schoolteacher.' He stroked her cheek with his hand and she saw it was shaking.

'Will you marry me, my sweet dove? Stay with me, be with me, bear my children and keep loving me even when I'm impossible, which is most of the time? I want you to be mine, completely mine, as I will be yours. I can't live without you, Aline. I love you, and I know now that I have never loved before.' He had said it, at last, when hope had faded, and in the depths of her something burst that was all-powerful, all-encompassing, healing all the pain.

She touched his hard, tanned face wonderingly, tracing the cruel mouth with a trembling finger. 'Yes, I'll marry you, Cord.'

His mouth came down on hers with such a devouring intensity that she marvelled at the iron control he had been exercising. She clung to him, scarcely able to believe that this strong, ruthless, powerful man was hers and that he wanted her for his wife. She was flushed and shaking when he let her go, moving her to arm's length with hands that weren't quite steady. 'I've never practised such restraint and I don't like it,' he growled softly, his eyes brilliant in his dark skin.

'You don't have to,' she said softly, loving him, wanting him.

'Oh, but I do.' There was a seriousness in his face now, and a slight hesitancy that touched her. 'This is going to be done right. You will come to me for the first time in Corsica, as a true Corsican bride, in a white dress and with fresh flowers in your hair. There will be a festival in the streets that will last for days and they will lead you to me in the little church in my village.'

She listened entranced as he sat with her again on the grass, taking her on his lap and stroking her silky blonde hair as he talked.

'We will sit in the village square after the ceremony and there will be much wine and merriment, and the first dance we will dance alone while all the men think how fortunate I am.' His eyes were dark and possessive on her fair skin.

'And then later, much later, when the air is full of music and love is heavy in the air, I shall carry you back to my house and to my bed. And then——' He paused to nuzzle her earlobe in a soft, sensual caress.

'And then?' She couldn't resist teasing him a little. 'What happens then?'

'And then I will possess you, utterly, completely, until the earth melts and the only thing that matters to you is me.' She shivered as his deep dark voice stroked her flesh. 'That is how it will be done, my little English dove.'

And it was.

Next Month's Romances

Each month you can choose from a wide variety of romance with Mills & Boon. Below are the new titles to look out for next month, why not ask either Mills & Boon Reader Service or your Newsagent to reserve you a copy of the titles you want to buy — just tick the titles you would like and either post to Reader Service or take it to any Newsagent and ask them to order your books.

Please save me the following titles:	Please tick	√
AN OUTRAGEOUS PROPOSAL	Miranda Lee	
RICH AS SIN	Anne Mather	
ELUSIVE OBSESSION	Carole Mortimer	
AN OLD-FASHIONED GIRL	Betty Neels	
DIAMOND HEART	Susanne McCarthy	
DANCE WITH ME	Sophie Weston	
BY LOVE ALONE	Kathryn Ross	
ELEGANT BARBARIAN	Catherine Spencer	
FOOTPRINTS IN THE SAND	Anne Weale	
FAR HORIZONS	Yvonne Whittal	
HOSTILE INHERITANCE	Rosalie Ash	
THE WATERS OF EDEN	Joanna Neil	
FATEFUL DESIRE	Carol Gregor	
HIS COUSIN'S KEEPER	Miriam Macgregor	
SOMETHING WORTH FIGHTING FOR	Kristy McCallum	
LOVE'S UNEXPECTED TURN	Barbara McMahon	

If you would like to order these books in addition to your regular subscription from Mills & Boon Reader Service please send £1.70 per title to: Mills & Boon Reader Service, P.O. Box 236, Croydon, Surrey, CR9 3RU, quote your Subscriber No:......................................
(If applicable) and complete the name and address details below. Alternatively, these books are available from many local Newsagents including W.H.Smith, J.Menzies, Martins and other paperback stockists from 12th February 1993.

Name:...
Address:...
....Post Code:...........................

To Retailer: If you would like to stock M&B books please contact your regular book/magazine wholesaler for details.

You may be mailed with offers from other reputable companies as a result of this application.
If you would rather not take advantage of these opportunities please tick box ☐

4 FREE

Romances
and 2 FREE gifts
just for you!

You can enjoy all the
heartwarming emotion of true love for FREE!
Discover the heartbreak and the happiness, the emotion and
the tenderness of the modern relationships in
Mills & Boon Romances.

We'll send you 4 captivating Romances as a special offer from
Mills & Boon Reader Service, along with the chance to have
6 Romances delivered to your door each month.

Claim your FREE books and gifts overleaf...

An irresistible offer from Mills & Boon

Here's a personal invitation from Mills & Boon Reader Service, to become a regular reader of Romances. To welcome you, we'd like you to have 4 books, a CUDDLY TEDDY and a special MYSTERY GIFT absolutely FREE.

Then you could look forward each month to receiving 6 brand new Romances, delivered to your door, postage and packing free! Plus our free Newsletter featuring author news, competitions, special offers and much more.

This invitation comes with no strings attached. You may cancel or suspend your subscription at any time, and still keep your free books and gifts.

It's so easy. Send no money now. Simply fill in the coupon below and post it to -
Reader Service, FREEPOST, PO Box 236, Croydon, Surrey CR9 9EL.

`NO STAMP REQUIRED`

Free Books Coupon

Yes! Please rush me 4 free Romances and 2 free gifts! Please also reserve me a Reader Service subscription. If I decide to subscribe I can look forward to receiving 6 brand new Romances each month for just £10.20, postage and packing free. If I choose not to subscribe I shall write to you within 10 days - I can keep the books and gifts whatever I decide. I may cancel or suspend my subscription at any time. I am over 18 years of age.

Ms/Mrs/Miss/Mr _____ EP31R

Address _____

_____

Postcode _____ Signature _____